AUTUMN LEAVES

A Collection of Poems

& Short Stories

Lynemouth Library

Writing Group

Copyright

Emma Eyers ©2025

Diane Gough ©2025

Kathleen Little ©2025

Christine McCluskey ©2025

Betty Mitcheson ©2025

Loraine Rutherford ©2025

David Swinton ©2025

Christine Waterson ©2025

Timothy Webb ©2025

Elaine B Wilson ©2025

All rights reserved

Introduction

This is our fourth anthology in less than three years, which shows the commitment and enthusiasm, necessary to write, continues to thrive.

Most of our poems and stories have been inspired from prompts and ideas suggested by members of the group or criteria laid down in competition, particularly a Furious Fiction challenge, entered monthly, in Australia!

As you will see, we all respond to the challenges in different ways and we hope that you enjoy the variety of stories included in this anthology.

Lynemouth Library Writing Group

Contents

Avenging the Innocent 1
Writers Block 22
The Old Village School 27
The House 29
Up the Stairs to Bedford 31
Stranger than Fiction? 33
Never Too Late 35
Common Ground 42
Sporting Rap 50
Yoga for Beginners 52
Theatre of War 56
Memories of Yesterday 58
Little Miss Muffett 60
I Should Sphynx So 62
Polly and Sukey 64
The Mystery at the Castle 70
The Staircase 75
The Owl 76
Groping in the Fog 79
Tea on the Train 81
The Bus Shelter 85
I'll Never Stop Saying 88
The Final Act 91

The Letter...*93*

Ah Yes, I Was Expecting You *96*

To bake or not to bake... that is the question.....................*100*

French Fried..*103*

After Three *105*

Armistice..*107*

Christmas...*117*

Friendship *119*

Acknowledgements *121*

Authors' Biographies..*123*

Avenging the Innocent

It was a dark and wet 7:00 am when Sergeant Reeves buzzed the intercom to flat 10 of the Ridgeway Housing Project. He heard the static click on the other end suggesting that the occupant of Flat 10 was opening the door to let him have access, despite having no clue as to who might be asking. There were no words spoken. It was Flat 4 he wanted access to, but he'd buzzed a few times and couldn't get an answer, which only helped to confirm his fears.

April Jackson hadn't been seen for a number of weeks now, according to her mother Jackie. It was Jackie who had rung the station to see if they could carry out a wellness check on her daughter. She would come, of course, but home for Jackie and her family was more than 200 miles away.

Sergeant Reeves made his way up the concrete steps, covered in an industrial red linoleum, to April's flat on the first floor. He was followed by PC Jade Rickerby, who was only a few weeks into her policing career, having previously been a men's barber. Handy, he thought!

Jade had never seen barbering as a long-term career, despite all the training and accolades she'd achieved in the barbering world. She'd grown uninspired over the last few years and needed more. It was her partner, Lindsay, who'd suggested Jade would be well suited to policing and well, here she was, following Sergeant Reeves to the flat of a suspected 'mis-per'. He was hardly 'Luther' from the TV series of the same name, but then she was no 'Sergeant Cawood' from TV's Happy Valley either, so, so far it was an even playing field.

Sergeant Reeves knocked a hard 'copper's knock' with his knuckles on the door and waited. Jade stood off to the side, listening for signs of movement inside the flat. Nothing. Sergeant Reeves lifted the letterbox of the uniform pillar-box red front door and was just about to call for the teenage occupant, but was thrown by the distinct smell of death emanating from the property.

After a minute or so, it was Jade who started to heave, "I have to get some air," she choked, having held her breath for as long as she was able.

Sergeant Reeves nodded. Sadly, the smell never got any easier to deal with, but he wouldn't tell Jade that, not just yet anyway. Stepping away from April's door to the top of the landing, Reeves made a call to the station.

"I'll need someone with the 'big red key' to get into this one," he told his colleague Graham Mac. "We'll also need the SOCO and an ambulance as quick as you can mate, thanks."

He disconnected the call and made to return to the foyer at the bottom of the stairs. He didn't hear the door across the hall from April's quietly open. The neighbour, a middle-aged woman still in her pyjamas, spotted Reeves' Police vest as he made his way down the stairs.

"Excuse me," she called after him to catch his attention.

Without turning, his deep police-trained voice boomed up the stairwell from the hollow passage below, "Hello," he called back, "How can I help?"

"If you would be so kind as to turn around, then I'll tell you..." the woman responded in a distinctly 'school ma'amish' tone.

Reeves sighed. A case of nosey neighbour, no doubt. He huffed, then turned to the young PC below him, "Go down and wait for the team while I deal with this, this bloody woman," he added under his breath. "Don't let anyone else through, we don't want to contaminate the scene."

Reeves turned back to the woman, "Right, Madam, shall we go inside?" He gestured to her open door.

Downstairs, Jade was worried. In training school they'd been told NOT to call SOCO, or an ambulance, until the property had been entered and a scene of crime or death had been discovered. Yes, there was an awful smell coming from the flat, but it may not be human. Still, she told herself, it wouldn't be her getting into bother, it would be that pompous, sexist, old sergeant.

Back upstairs Reeves followed the woman into the flat. "Right Mrs..?" he raised his eyebrows questioningly.

"Brown, Sergeant, and it's Ms, if you please."

"Of course it is," Reeves thought. "My apologies. Right, Ms. Brown, how might I be of assistance?"

"Well, Sergeant, I do hope you can help. I've been phoning the Police Station for the past three weeks, more so this last week. I told the officer that I was becoming worried about my young neighbour. I haven't seen her out and about, which is unusual. She always had time for a quick chat. I've noticed men arriving at the flat; swarthy looking men, who usually came around midnight, or later."

"Mrs... sorry, Ms Brown, young lasses these days keep later hours, and have many friends of different cultures. What makes you so concerned?"

"Sergeant... I told you, I've not seen April around... until five nights ago that is. I heard her door open and hurried footsteps from the stairwell. I looked out of the front window to see April scurrying across the road. She looked in a terrible hurry, glancing nervously over her shoulder. She was dishevelled and had a small rucksack on her back. To me, it appeared she was attempting to escape from something or someone, but the officer didn't seem at all perturbed. He said he would note my concerns!"

"Well," Reeves started...

"These past few days I've noticed an unsavoury smell emanating from April's flat," Ms. Brown interrupted, "now perhaps you'll do something!"

When SOCO arrived, Sergeant Reeves took their initial report and called out senior help. DCI Wilson duly arrived a few minutes later. Unlike the stereotypical female DCI, Wilson was young and well dressed in a classic business suit with medium heels. She could, were the light suitably muted and the onlooker without their usual spectacles, be considered passably attractive in a quirky sort of way.

DCI Wilson surveyed the partially decomposed body.

"What have we got Bobby?" Her question was directed to the lead pathologist in the SOCO team, a middle-aged Scottish doctor with a long line in tattoos and a short temper.

"You'll know when I know. Male, probably mid-40s, wallet with ID in pocket. Dead just less than a week. Blunt force trauma to the head might, and I stress might, be the cause of death. Anything else will have to wait for the PM."

DCI Wilson knew from experience not to push it, so returned to the Station to assemble the case.

Staff shortages meant her 'team' would consist only of the half-wit Sergeant Reeves and the wet-behind-the-ears ex-barber PC Rickerby. The DCI knew she would have to rely on her own intellect to solve this one.

"Right Rickerby make yourself useful, put what we've got so far on the white board."

"Yes ma'am," came the overly keen reply. The PC began writing associated names on the board. "Ma'am, deceased ID shows a William Coppit, 45, works at Build It Engineering. Flat belongs to an April Jackson, who a neighbour saw leaving hurriedly several days ago. Miss Jackson apparently used to get male callers in the late evening so maybe a 'working girl'?"

"Facts Rickerby, just the facts, that last bit is pure speculation," Wilson interjected briskly.

"Yes Ma'am, sorry Ma'am. No address for deceased on the system Ma'am."

"Possible deceased Rickerby, possible deceased. We don't yet have positive ID. Sergeant Reeves, your thoughts?"

"Well Ma'am we need to trace April Jackson as soon as possible and find out what relationship, if any, she had with the victim. We also need to know as much about William Coppit as we can find Ma'am."

"Good work Reeves. Right, here's the plan. PC Rickerby, go back to the scene and interview as many neighbours as you can find. I want details, all the details, just write them down and don't try to think too hard. We'll have more to go on when the full PM is in. I'll start with Coppit's place of work from the ID card, Build It Engineering. Sergeant Reeves, with me."

At that DCI Wilson strode out of the room. The hunt was on...

The Receptionist at Build It Engineering looked startled to see a uniformed sergeant and even more concerned, when DCI Wilson produced her warrant card and asked for William Coppit. Sergeant Reeves looked surprised too, considering the man is dead! But not only were his eyebrows raised, his mouth gaped open when the Receptionist said, "I'll put a call out for him, if you'd like to take a seat," indicating the waiting area.

Wilson, looked smug and Reeves, very puzzled. As they moved away from the desk, the Receptionist, her eyes following them, pressed the button on her call system, "Will Coppit, please report to Reception, Will Coppit to Reception, thank you."

The Sergeant went to speak, but the DCI held up her hand and put her finger to her lips. Within a few minutes, the lift door opened and an overalled man in his early fifties stepped out, heading for the Receptionist. She nodded in their direction and instead of looking concerned, the man smiled and came towards them.

"Don't tell me, you've found my wallet? Just when I thought I'd never get it back."

"We have found your wallet Mr Coppit," the DCI said, "but perhaps you can tell us where you lost it."

"That's the problem, I'm not really sure. It could have been at the night club or on the way home."

The DCI took out her pocket book and pen, "Which night club, Sir?"

"The Blue Heron, I go there to play poker."

"When was the last time you had it?"

"Last Friday, when I paid to get into the casino."

"And how did you get home?"

"I walked; you can never get a cab at that time of morning," he said with a wry grin.

"Where do you live?"

"7 Ridgeway."

Again, Sergeant Reeves' eyebrows shot up his forehead and his mouth fell open, "That's where," he began, but hastily clammed up when he saw DCI Wilson's look of disapproval.

"There wasn't much in the wallet; I didn't have a very good night," Will said ruefully. "I've cancelled the cards and been issued another ID for here, so it's no big deal."

"Do you know an April Jackson, Mr Coppit?" DCI Wilson enquired.

"I don't think so, should I?"

"She lives…" Sergeant Reeves began, but DCI Wilson interrupted, "Perhaps you would call at the station after work, Mr Coppit, so we can return your wallet?"

"Great, thanks," Will said, looking pleased.

DCI Wilson strode to the door with Reeves sheepishly following. Once in the car, the DCI exploded, "There was no need for you to say anything! You nearly gave the game away!"

"What game?" Sergeant Reeves asked querulously.

"That he, William Coppit, lives in the same block of flats as our missing person and where a dead man's been found in possession of *his* ID!"

"But that's true!" the Sergeant argued.

"Yes, but he didn't need to know that – not yet! We'll interview him again when he comes for his wallet. For now, we need to concentrate on finding April Jackson."

'I think I suggested that about an hour ago,' thought Reeves rather miffed, but instead said, "and find out the identity of 'John Doe'?"

"Quite," DCI Wilson said flatly, ending any further conversation.

"OK, so far, we have established that our victim is not Will Coppit and Rickerby's interviews with the neighbours haven't brought anything to light that can help us. So, we need to see if the DNA of the deceased matches with anything already on the system. We may be lucky. Rickerby, I'd like you to do that and to check CCTV from Ridgeway. See if we can trace where April went after rushing from the flat. Reeves you will come with me. I think it's time to give Jackie Jackson a visit and the Blue Heron. I want to examine their CCTV."

For most of the three- and three-quarter hour journey from Birmingham to Newcastle, Reeves and Wilson travelled in silence and when there was conversation, it was stilted. Rickerby on the other hand was thoroughly enjoying herself, utterly convinced that this was better than being a barber. The DNA database had brought up a match with one Vincent Young. Previously, he had been charged with dangerous driving and he had been accused of inappropriate sexual conduct but that had been, subsequently, withdrawn. The interesting thing was that he lived in Newcastle. 'Was this just another coincidence?' thought Rickerby.

Encouraged by her findings, she set about plotting possible routes that April would have taken and identified the siting of

CCTV cameras from Ridgeway. This task initially felt overwhelming until she started to apply logic to it. Rickerby decided that, if she was in April's position, she would head for either the train station or bus station. The neighbour had already identified her on the CCTV camera near her home, so Rickerby knew what she was looking for. If there was a patron saint of Police Constables, he was definitely looking after Rickerby because on her first attempt, she managed to track April to Birmingham New Street station and onto platform 9, where she boarded a train to Newcastle.

As they approached Newcastle, Wilson seriously hoped it wasn't going to be a wasted journey and they'd find no-one at the house. She had considered phoning ahead but didn't want to alert Jackie, in case she tipped off her daughter. When she received Rickerby's update, she was even more pleased that she'd not forewarned them, as it appeared likely April was in Newcastle.

Reeves pulled up in front of a tidy 1930s semi-detached. The front door was answered quickly by a thin woman with early signs of grey hair. Her complexion suggested she was a smoker.

"Jackie Jackson? I am DI Wilson and this is Sergeant Reeves. We would like to talk to you about April. Would you mind if we come in?"

Reeves noticed the panic in her eyes as she ushered them in. Wilson took the lead, asking her when she had last seen her daughter, general questions about their relationship and April's character. Reeves took the opportunity to glance around the room and he noted a photograph of April with another girl who, judging by the similarities in appearance, could be April's sister. Feeling slightly redundant, except for taking some brief notes, he asked if he could use the toilet; it had been a long journey. Wilson glared at him, but before waiting to hear directions, he left the room and headed upstairs.

Stopping on a landing halfway up the stairs, there was, as he thought, a window leading onto the garage roof. When he'd been looking at the photograph, which was placed below the mirror above the mantelpiece, he'd glimpsed a reflection of something moving in the mirror. The glass panel door to the living room gave a view of the stairs. The window on the landing looked as if it had been opened recently; the ornament was in the corner of the sill and while the window was closed, the latch was off. Reeves continued to the bathroom and peered out of that window. It gave a view of the back garden and the summerhouse.

"Thank you, Mrs Jackson. That will be all for now," said DI Wilson.

"What a lovely garden, you have," remarked Reeves as they were leaving the house. Wilson glared. "I love gardening. Do you mind if I have a look at the back garden?" he asked, but was already making his way there. "That's a lovely display of lavender," he continued, heading towards the summerhouse.

As Wilson registered his direction, she increased her pace until both of them were standing in front of the door. Reeves opened it and peered in.

"April, we need to talk to you," he declared.

Back at the station, Wilson directed Reeves to visit the Blue Heron and check the CCTV, while she and Rickerby interviewed April.

When Reeves returned, Will Coppit was sitting in reception, waiting to collect his wallet. Reeves put his head into the interview room, "Ma'am," he interrupted, gesturing for her to leave the room.

"Interview suspended at 18.45."

"OK Reeves, what have you got?"

"Both Victor Young and Will Coppit appeared on the CCTV and were playing at the same table at one point. It's a bit hazy but it looks as if Will dropped his wallet. Later there's a shot of Victor bending down to pick something up."

"So, he didn't steal it?"

"Doesn't look like it Ma'am."

"Is our Victor a good citizen who was trying to return the wallet to Mr Coppit?"

"But I did find out," Reeves ploughed on, "that Will Coppit recently had a run of bad luck. Something has gone on with his daughter, which has led to all sorts of mental health problems and the difficulties with the daughter have led to the break-up of his marriage."

"Maybe that's why he's living in Ridgeway - accommodation that a young woman can afford. Mmm, Reeves you come in with me this time. Rickerby, can you offer Mr Coppit coffee and say that we will be with him shortly?"

"OK April. Let's start again. Do you know a Will Coppit?"

"Will from Build It Engineering? Yes."

Reeves and Wilson looked puzzled. "Not from number 7 Ridgeway?" asked Wilson.

"No. He's one of the bosses at the factory where I'm doing my placement. Most of the time we have nothing to do with them, but he was around one night shift and we got talking. He seemed like a nice man."

"OK. Do you know a Victor Young?"

April looked down.

"April, we need you to answer the question." Wilson pushed a photograph of the dead body surrounded in blood across the table.

"Yes, but I didn't do it."

"Tell us what happened, April."

Slowly, April spoke, "I was returning from my night shift and when I was putting the key in the front door, I saw Victor Young walking along the corridor. I recognized him at once. I don't think he knew who I was until he got closer. I was still fumbling to open the door, as my hands were shaking, and he came up close to me. He stank of drink. 'Well, well, if it isn't April. This is a surprise,' he said, 'It's been a long time. Are you going to let me in?' He took the key out of my hand, turned the lock and walked in. I told him I wanted him to go, but he wouldn't listen. He then started asking about my sister. I don't know if he knew or not but he was making me mad."

"What about your sister?" Wilson interrupted.

April looked down at the floor for a long time.

"Victor raped my sister. He was a friend of the family and our parents were away. He popped in to see if we were OK. I was with a friend and when I got back, I found Susie distraught. She told me what had happened. I said that we ought to go to the Police. She was scared to, but we did the following day. The day after, our parents returned and we told them what'd happened. Mum was horrified, but Dad told Susie to stop making things up; that Victor was a good friend of the family and that she should not make such awful allegations, as they could have serious consequences for Victor. He called Susie a 'slapper'. Dad made her withdraw her statement to the Police. Mum and Dad were never the same after that and Mum divorced him a year later. Susie was never the same either. She also blamed herself for the break-up of the family and committed suicide six months later."

"You have very good reason to dislike Victor Young."

"Yes. But I did not kill him."

"Carry on telling us what happened the night before he was found dead."

"He started getting closer to me and trying to kiss me. He said he knew what the Jackson girls were like and that they liked it. I was furious. I pushed him away and he grabbed me by the hair. It was then that I 'kneed' him in the groin – really hard. I think the drink had made him wobbly on his feet because he stumbled and let go of me to steady himself and cope with the pain. I ran into the bathroom and locked the door. I wasn't in there long when I heard a really loud thump. I didn't know what to do because I didn't know if it was safe for me to go and look. I must have stayed in the bathroom another ten minutes or so. There'd been no sound from the living room. I looked in, he was lying on the floor with blood around his head. I was so scared. I just threw some things in my rucksack and left as quickly as I could," April said between heavy sobs.

"You must realise how this looks. A man, whom you had good reason to hate, is found dead in your apartment and you ran away."

"I know but I didn't kill him. Honest. I ran because I knew what people would think."

They sat in silence for a while. Finally, Wilson asked, "What did you talk about with Will Coppit on your night shift that made you think he was a nice man?"

Reeves looked at her curiously.

"I was upset because it was the anniversary of Susie's death. He asked me what was wrong. He was so easy to talk to and seemed to understand. I told him what had happened."

"Did you mention the name Victor Young to him?"

"Um, I don't know. Maybe. Uh, that's right I showed him a picture. I was showing him Susie, but all I had was one of a family gathering and Victor was in it. I said he was the man I was talking about."

As Wilson and Reeves made their way to Will Coppit, both were trying to make sense of what they had just heard, but refrained from discussion.

"Sorry to keep you waiting, Mr Coppit," said Wilson with a smile.

Coppit opened his mouth to comment, but Wilson rolled on. "While you're here, we would just like to ask you a few questions about an incident that occurred at Ridgeway."

"I saw the Police about and the tape, but I don't know what it's got to do with me."

"We're making routine enquiries with all the neighbours and since you're here, we might as well do it now."

"Does the name April Jackson mean anything to you?"

"You've already asked me that question and I've already told you, no."

"What about the name Victor Young?" Reeves sat quietly scrutinizing Will for any tell-tell signs.

"No. Don't know anyone of that name. Now can I go?"

"You live at 7 Ridgeway, is that right?"

Will nodded.

"How well do you know your neighbours?"

"I say 'hello' in passing. I haven't been there that long – just a few months since my wife kicked me out."

"Have you ever said 'hello' to the occupant of number 4?"

"I might have done. Am I being suspected of something?"

"April Jackson lives at number 4 and another interesting thing is that she's on placement at Build It Engineering. That is where you work, isn't it? Now I'll ask you again. Do you know April Jackson, Mr Coppit?"

Will sat in silence. Finally, he said, "If she's on placement, she'll be one of our degree apprentices who work mainly on night shift. I work normal office hours."

"April knows you. You spoke to her on one night shift."

Will shuffled in his seat, "Oh, so that's April. Yes, I remember now. Sorry. Nice girl. Had a hard time."

"Let us jog your mind further," interjected Reeves as he pushed forward a photo of Will talking to Victor at the Blue Heron. "This was taken from the CCTV. Now can we start getting some straight answers?"

"I don't have to stay here, you know."

"That's true but we'll just call you in again," smiled Wilson.

"I would like a solicitor."

"Very well, that can be arranged."

Two hours later, when the solicitor finally arrived, Wilson and Reeves were tired and wanted a resolution.

"Now let's look at what we have. Victor Young, to whom you're seen talking, is murdered in a flat, in the same apartment block where you live. The flat belongs to an April Jackson who works at your place of employment and with whom you have spoken. You seem to be a common denominator, Mr Coppit," pointed out Wilson.

"It doesn't make me guilty of anything."

"Why did your wife kick you out?"

"My client doesn't have to answer that."

Wilson nodded.

"What has been wrong with your daughter?"

"This has got nothing to do with her. Leave her out if it," Coppit replied before his solicitor could interject.

"That seems to have hit a nerve."

"I said, leave her out of this. She's been through enough."

"And what was that? You see, we feel that for some reason, you're very protective of your daughter and when you heard April's story you felt similar protection. You saw an opportunity to bring some justice."

"That's nonsense- all of it. You've got nothing on me."

"If you weren't trying to protect April, what was going on?"

Coppit remains silent, his jaw moving, his mouth clamped shut.

"What do you think Reeves?"

Reeves was pleasantly surprised to get an opportunity to speak and measuredly said, "Has this got something to do with your daughter? Did Victor hurt her?"

At that, Coppit suddenly stood up and leaned over the desk towards Reeves. His solicitor hastily grabbed Coppit by the arm and talked him back into his seat.

"I think you've hit a nerve there," observed Wilson as she looked at her Sergeant.

He nodded, feeling rather pleased.

"Maybe we should bring your daughter in for questioning; find out if she knows Victor Young."

'Ouch,' thought, Reeves. 'This woman knows how to hit below the belt.'

"NO!!" Coppit yelled, "OK, I'll talk as long as you promise not to contact my daughter."

Wilson and Reeves exchanged glances, then Wilson nodded to Coppit.

"My daughter was sexually attacked and has suffered mental health issues ever since. She's just not the same girl; she even had to be sectioned on one occasion. When April told me about her sister, I thought it all sounded so familiar. She told me it had taken place in Newcastle, so initially, I didn't think there was any connection, until I saw the photograph of Victor. I recognised him from the Blue Heron. It was then I wondered if he was the perpetrator. I took some photos of Victor and showed them to my daughter. She didn't say a word, but started shaking from head to foot and when she pushed the image away, I knew."

"So, you and April devised a plan?" prompted Reeves.

"No. I haven't spoken to April since that night at work. Anyway, who would come up with such an unreliable plan? There was no guarantee that Victor would pick up the wallet or choose to return it, if that's what he was doing. It was all serendipitous; the fact he chose, I presume, to return the wallet at the time April returned home, and when I was just leaving my apartment to search for it. That was what was so amazing; I saw him open her flat door and walk in, so I picked up the metal doorstop that I have in my hallway and stood in the corridor outside April's apartment. I heard raised voices and scuffling and then a door close sharply. It was then I went in. Victor was standing with his back to the front door. I hit him and left."

Silence filled the room. Eventually Wilson said, "Will Coppit, I am arresting you for the murder of Victor Young."

Back in the briefing room, Wilson updated Rickerby on events and congratulated the team on a good result.

"A good job well done and one that couldn't have been achieved without all our efforts. Rickerby, can you, please, go and tell April Jackson that she's free to go."

As Wilson and Reeves made their way to the station exit, they saw April walking out with Jackie, arm in arm.

"Do you think that she really didn't have anything to do with it?" asked Reeves.

Wilson shrugged her shoulders, "We have a confession - case closed. And maybe," she said looking at the mother and daughter, "that family has gone through enough."

Diane Gough, Christine McCluskey, Chris Waterson,
Timothy Webb and Elaine B Wilson

Writers Block

My wife advises me, repeatedly, that, when I am asked what I do, I should tell people that I am an author. For a while I did follow her advice, but I found all too often people receiving the information would reply with the socially acceptable question, "and what have you written?" which would immediate be followed with the supplementary question, "anything I am likely to have read?" I reply with a knowing smile and a non-committal "Oh, I doubt it," and failed to correct their assumption that my work must fall into the area of academia. My luck finally ran out, at one of those little drinks' parties, so beloved by my wife and universally detested by me, when a Professor of something or other from a University I remember as a Polytechnic, allowed a fatal combination of politeness and curiosity to formulate further investigation. Within seconds the truth was out; I am an unpublished author.

Why is it society declines to take seriously the unpublished author while readily accepting and even commiserating with, for instance, the out of work actor? Authors submit articles and stories in the same way that actors attend auditions. An actor who fails to be cast can rest assured that it was because he was too tall, or the wrong age and all his chums will offer condolences and assure him that the part on offer was beneath him and the Director couldn't recognise talent if he tripped over it.

And what about Artists? They smear paint on a piece of paper or canvas and immediately they have something to show and sell. Let's face it there are plenty of myopic philanthropists in search of a picture to cover over an inconvenient damp patch on a wall. What can the unpublished author do? Paste pages of his unpublished opus on a wall?

Unfortunately, these thoughts are at the front of my mind as I climb the stairs to my study. Routine, that's the secret of success. Routine. Regular working hours just like a normal job. Regular start and finish times and a minimum number of words each day. That is the discipline emphasised, repeatedly, in the book entitled 'So you want to be a writer' thoughtfully purchased for me by my wife as a birthday present last year. "If you have any hope of becoming a published author you need discipline", the Authors words ring in my ears as I sit at the keyboard at my regular daily start time of 10.00 – well there has to be some advantage of being self-employed. The trouble is I sat all day yesterday without adding a single word and I can't think of anything today either. Pull yourself together. Discipline. Get writing. Access the muse.

Commence the routine. Switch on the PC, wait patiently while electricity awakens the incomprehensible collection of circuitries that somehow makes the whole thing work. Two or three clicks of the mouse and, why is it called a mouse? Well, I suppose it had to be called something, and someone must have decided an anthropomorphic name is as good as anything else. Anyway, a few clicks of the mouse and I will be exactly where I left off at 4.30 the day before yesterday. The final full stop of the day, and there it stands as a sentinel preventing the words slipping off the screen. Beyond the full stop the screen lies waiting. Then the screen goes blank. Why are there no little lights confirming the computer is on?

Coffee, then I'll sort it out.

Standing gazing out of the kitchen window waiting for the kettle to boil I realise that the garden has imperceptibly made the move from being a wild garden, nature reserve into an embarrassing wilderness of knee-high grass supporting spindly bushes. That's the problem with being a writer, I have no time for the normal things in life. Good thing the garden can't be seen from the front of the house. I'll sort it at the weekend. Perhaps I should build a writing room at the bottom of the garden. Ok, so it would just be a shed but a posh shed and working down there would enable me to say that I go to work each day rather than working from home. I'll Google sheds when I'm back in the study, before I start work.

The kettle seems to be taking its time. It's still cold. It's not working. Nothing seems to be working. All the power must be off. Is it just our house or the whole street? I'll just pop next door and check. Opening the front door a thought hits me. John will be at work so Marion will be alone. For a split second, the prospect of being alone with Marion excites and tantalises, but reality forces its unwelcome way into my thoughts. I close the door with me still on the inside. If I nip upstairs, and look out of our spare bedroom window, I can see into Marion's kitchen. With guilt, and a slight twinge of unrealistic expectation, I squint round the curtains. There is Marion sitting at her kitchen table drinking a cup of coffee listening to the radio. So, it must be a fuse or circuit breaker or whatever they have in fuse boxes these days. Until I sort the fuse there can be no work, no computer and, more worryingly, no coffee. Five hours without coffee, I don't think so. Where is the fuse box?

Armed with screwdrivers, pliers and a very old card of fuse wire from my trusty toolbox the search begins. How can it be this difficult to find the fuse box? Will this quest prove the old maxim that you find things in the last place you look? What a silly saying. Of course you find things in the last place you look. You stop looking when you find it. The trouble is, this time, I am rapidly running out of places for the builder to have hidden a fuse box so it may well be found it in the last place I look, only because there is nowhere else to look.

How can I have lived in a house for seven years and not know where they fitted the fuse box? When, eventually, I do locate it I instantly understand why I had no idea where it had been fitted in the house and why I have had so much trouble finding it. The little box had been covered by the unbelievably expensive wallpaper my wife chose to decorate our hallway, rendering it invisible to all but the most persistent questor. What kind of tradesman papers over the lid of a fuse box? How am I supposed to repair a blown fuse without ripping the paper? Standing uneasily on a kitchen chair I discover to my delight that I had employed a quality tradesman, and he had anticipated the need of access to the inner workings of the fuse box and the lid drops down on its plastic hinge without any damage to the surrounding decoration. Now let's have a look.

Why am I lying in confused muddle of arms and legs on the hall floor. Now I'm no medical expert but even I know my arm should not be that shape. What is that strange smell? Have I fallen and broken my arm? I need to get to hospital. Call for an ambulance. Where is my phone? Ah yes, in my pocket. Which pocket? The one I am lying on, which helps to explain the pain in by buttock. Bit of a struggle to extract it due to having only one working arm. Just about to bring the phone to life when I see my reflection in the screen. My hair, what is left of it, is standing straight up and smoking. 999. Ambulance please. Hello, I think I need an Ambulance. What's the problem? Well, you see, it's a bit of a long story. I've got writer's block...

David Swinton

The Old Village School

I see in my mind the old school
In the village, as it
Used to look years ago.
The small playground and the
Tiny rooms, which sheltered
Us as we learnt.

Generations before us had passed
Through that school, the old
Somewhat homely desks must
Have witnessed many years
Of learning, under that old roof.

The church across the road
Would have seen many school
Services, harvest festivals with
Yellow corn and apples green.
Christmas services, with choirs
From the school.

Many years have passed now
Since I saw the old school
Shut its doors on pupils for the
Last time. A new school further
Down the village took its place.
Larger classrooms, without the
Homely feel.

The old school now stands
Quiet, the children's voices gone
From within the now silent walls.
A private residence, a monument
To the village's past.

Kathleen Little

The House

I'm a little piece of history. I've stood for a few hundred years, seeing plenty of the family come and go. People think that houses can't talk and we can't tell stories, but we can.

The same family lived in me for several generations, but the day they got taken I didn't know.

It started when the sun was just beginning to rise, that awful morning. It was a Sunday, so none of the family had to be up quite as early as normal. Praying was illegal if you were believing in the wrong God.

I felt something heavy banging on my door, harder than anyone had ever done before. I felt my wood starting to splinter.

My family, clearly panicking, tried to get out, even though they were just in their night clothes.

"You must all come with us," shouted the uniformed men, looking menacing in their black clothing with their swastikas on show.

I could hear and feel it, as they got dragged outside and bundled into some waiting vehicles, not even having had time to grab anything.

I felt something shatter inside me, as I heard the vehicles leaving. I didn't know what their fate was going to be. I still don't know.

They moved a displaced family into me next, who treated me like they didn't care about my internal pieces, like the furniture. They kept what they were allowed to help themselves, and the men in black tore everything else out of me.

Months passed by, with the family not caring other than making sure I didn't fall down. All I know is I got woken up by the sound of my friend over the road exploding, when an eerie whistling sound shot out of the sky, ending with a boom and my friend suddenly disappearing.

My new family clambered out of me and ran for the shelter, leaving me to the mercy of the fiery booms from the sky.

I could hear wails and sirens and all sorts of noises, then when I was shouting (in house language) for my friend, there was an eerie whistle above me and then a boom. It felt like the whole of my insides were being dragged outside, then blackness claimed me.

Nobody will remember any of us from this street, none of us houses made it through the whistle bangs that night. I just hope my humans who got taken by the black uniforms will one day return. It's my final wish.

Emma Eyers

Up the Stairs to Bedford

Cosy and warm. This bed's got to be the best I've ever slept in. Pity I haven't got it for long. I heard the nurse talking to Stanley. They always talk in that whisper but you can hear every word they say. Mmm, when I move my foot just a little bit I can reach a lovely cool part of the sheet, which I quite like as I know I'm not going to be cold. The covers are quite snug but not heavy. I can't move under anything heavy. Well, I can't even manage to lift my eyelids now. Anyway, I prefer to keep my eyes shut so they all think I'm unconscious and then I can listen to what they're saying about me. The nurse keeps saying soothing things to Stanley. Perhaps she fancies him. Ha. She can have him. He can pop the question when I've popped off.

I never really loved him. It was Ronnie I loved and he went and married my sister. I've spent a lot of years hating the pair of them. Oh, what's this now? Ah, one of those sponges to wet my lips. I always wanted Ronnie to kiss my lips. Ooh, I would get butterflies in the pit of my stomach imagining it. That must be how it feels when it's real and you want that person so close. My head upon the pillow next to his. My head will leave its shape in this pillow when I'm gone. Until the next dying soul comes along. That's a good point, Mavis, they'll be wanting this bed so you shouldn't keep them waiting too long. There's light shining on the counterpane. I can't tell whether it's from the sun or from a lamp, but it's casting the shape of an arrow at the foot of the bed. That's funny. It could be saying this way to see the incredible shrinking woman. Free to enter.

I wonder whether the boys will come. Always so rough and untidy they were. I could never love them the way my parents loved me. My mother hardly ever got cross with me, not even when I wet the bed. I won't wet this bed though, as I have a catheter in. The nurse who smells of garlic is moving me now. If you get bed sores you can sue them, apparently. The authorities I mean, not the bed sores. Silly old woman. Up the stairs to Bedford. Night night, Mummy. Up the stairs to Bedford. Night night, Daddy.

Choking a bit now. Sounds like the old death rattle. A rushing sound in my ears and then floating. Our mattress was called Dreamland but it never was. This one should be R.I.P Mavis.

Daddy told me that Mavis meant a thrush, and he called me his little bird. I'm coming now, Mummy and Daddy, up the stairs to Bedford. Yes, hold my hand...

"She's gone now," the nurse said.

Loraine Rutherford

Stranger than Fiction?

My youngest son Graeme is a sculptor. He began his career in a small workshop that quickly became too small for the large items he was capable of producing and moved into much bigger workshop which is equipped with all manner of lifting gear and stone carving equipment. Around the walls are pictures and sketches of projects of past present and future work and in the corner of the workshop next to the office and covered thick in stone dust is a carved portrait stone of the ex-Newcastle United and England football manager Sir Bobby Robson.

A few years ago, he was commissioned by the Sir Bobby Robson foundation to do a sculpture for the memorial park which is in the shadow of St James Park and near Strawberry Place. The sculpture he designed is in five pieces in the shape of an arc which resembles the arc of the Tyne Bridge and each of the stones is carved with aspects of Sir Bobby's career. The project was no easy task as the area it is set is on a slope but it all came together and the day came for the official unveiling.

All manner of Newcastle dignitaries were there. Lady Elsie, Sir Bobby's wife, the Mayoress of Newcastle, Alan Pardew Newcastle manager as well as other representatives of the club.

The Mayoress made her speech but also declared that Graeme was a lifelong Newcastle supporter which astonished his friends and family as Graeme was a Sunderland red and white through and through.

Apart from the announcement of Graeme's football team all seemed to go well. As it turned out Graeme had told Lady Elsie that he was a Sunderland fan and she had confided that her and Sir Bobby when they were first married used to go to Newcastle one week and Sunderland the next!

Stranger than fiction? Who would believe that the memorial to Sir Bobby Robson, one of Newcastle and England's best managers and sited within the shadow of St James Park, was designed and carved by a Mackem?

Betty Mitcheson

Never Too Late

"Hello," the young man said simply.

"Hello," I respond uncertainly.

I'd barely heard the knock on the door; it was just a gentle tap, but I was on my way out, so opened it without thinking. His smile was vaguely familiar and there was a look in his eyes I couldn't quite fathom.

"Nan, it's me, Michael."

It took me a millisecond for this to register and realise this was my grandson, who I hadn't seen since he was a toddler.

"Michael?" I repeat hesitantly, thinking maybe I've died and gone to heaven, as this scenario has played out in my mind so often.

"Yes Nan, I'm sorry it's taken me so long."

Realising we're standing on the doorstep, in full view of nosey neighbours and looking like strangers, I stand aside, inviting him in. As soon as he's over the threshold, I slam the door shut and as one, we embrace. What a wonderful moment; am I dreaming? I release my grip on him and place my hands either side of his face, looking into his clear blue eyes, and give him a kiss on the cheek. He doesn't flinch, as he might have when he was a little boy, but returns the affection.

"Is it really you?" I ask him.

"It's really me, Nan. I've been wanting to find you for years, but it's only now I've been able to."

"Why, what's happened?"

"It's a long story, have you got time?"

"I've got all the time in the world. I'll put the kettle on."

We settle with cups of coffee and a plate of chocolate biscuits, sitting either side of the kitchen table; his hand covers mine and I see the serious look, even though he's smiling.

"Dad died a couple of months ago Nan, and I wanted to find you to tell you face to face, not by email or over the phone."

"I know," I say quietly, "your mum's sister, Jean let me know by letter."

Michael looks surprised, "I had no idea you were in touch with her," he says.

"I wasn't; I think she just thought I should know. The letter went to my old address, but got sent on. She invited me to the funeral, but it came too late. I wouldn't have gone anyway, it would look like I was dancing on his grave!"

"You'll know then, that it was sudden, from a heart attack."

I nod, but say nothing. The news had come as a shock and even though we'd not spoken in years, he was still my son and I couldn't forget him.

"It was my fault," Michael said steadily, "I challenged him about you. I wanted to know what had happened; why you never visited; why we never heard from you."

"Did he tell you?"

"No, he died before he could explain, but when I was sorting through his papers, I found letters and cards you'd sent, that I never received."

"I stopped sending them," I say shamefully.

"I'm not surprised, you must have thought me awfully ungrateful."

"No, I think I knew you weren't getting them, so there seemed little point."

"I've finished Uni and I want you at my graduation," Michael says abruptly.

"Maybe that's not…" I stutter before he interrupts.

"Nan, for so many years you've been missing from my life. I didn't even know if you were still alive, but I remember you looking after me. You read me stories, we sang nursery rhymes, we went to the park. You were always there and then suddenly, you weren't!"

"It was complicated," I begin, but Michael interrupts again.

"No, it wasn't; I heard Dad send you away, saying he never wanted to see you again, but I never knew why and I was too afraid to ask."

"I fell out with your mother. We had words and she made him choose between us."

"I know that now, but why didn't you come back into our lives after she left him?"

"He didn't ask me."

In truth, we hadn't spoken for such a long time, I imagine the conversation would have been very difficult for both of us. Michael's dad, because of pride and not wanting to ask for help and me, attempting to heal a rift that had got bigger and bigger over the years.

Michael was looking at me, clearly struggling to think of something to say, to find an explanation. Eventually, he said, "Can we put the past behind us Nan?"

"I'd like nothing better Michael, but I doubt everyone will forgive and forget."

"Who's everyone? No one else really matters except you."

"Aren't you in touch with your mother?"

"No, she left and never came back. She ruined so many people's lives; yours, mine, her family's; they never forgave her for running off with the American, who also left his family for her, so there's even more people with good reason to hate her."

"Hate is a very strong word, Michael. Do you really hate her?"

"I don't love her, that's for sure, and dislike intensely is pretty much hate, isn't it?"

"I'm so sorry it's come to that. I had to walk away when there seemed to be no conciliation. Believe me, I did try, but at the time, no one was listening."

"I'm listening now, Nan. Please tell me what happened."

I take a deep breath, knowing full well Michael might well judge me as harshly as his parents. Over the intervening years, I have questioned my reactions and deeply regret what occurred, but it wasn't all my doing and I have to tell my story so Michael can make up his own mind.

Everyone was thrilled when Nancy, Michael's mum, became pregnant as it was very unexpected. She and Robert, my son, had shown no intentions of starting a family, as they were both very successful business people and enjoyed all the trappings; foreign holidays, meals out, entertaining lavishly in their grand house. Although surprised, I was pleased for them and offered to help in any way I could. That was my first mistake. Instead of embracing parenthood and all the responsibilities that entails, Robert and Nancy took advantage of my offer and totally relied on me to look after Michael.

At first, I didn't realise what was happening; I was so besotted with him, being my only grandchild and, astonishingly, it didn't occur to me that no one else seemed to be getting involved. I was a widow, but Nancy had parents and siblings who I should have thought would want to play a part in his life, yet rarely did.

Things came to a head when I announced that I needed a break and was going to visit an old friend. Nancy's reaction was beyond belief, practically accusing me of desertion, with a very heavy dose of guilt thrown in! She more or less told me I couldn't go, as she was about to embark on a new venture in America.

I almost caved in, but her unreasonable tirade only made me more resolute. I had, single-handedly, looked after her child nearly every week day for almost three years; the only time off I'd had was when they went away on holiday and even then, I'd spent time at the house, spring cleaning! Not only an unpaid nanny, but an unpaid cleaner as well. It was of course, my own stupid fault, but I thought they were grateful for my help and in fairness, I was happy to fill my days being useful.

Disappointingly, Robert sided with Nancy and suddenly, I was surplus to requirements as they wasted no time getting Michael into a nursery and hiring a cleaner.

I went on my break, enjoying a few days respite in the company of my non-judgemental friend, who listened patiently to my account of what had happened. She agreed I'd been blind-sided to their selfishness, because of my love for Michael, and I returned determined to make my feelings known in the hope we could move on amicably.

Sadly, that discussion never took place, as the door was very firmly slammed shut behind me after the argument that Michael overheard. I wrote letters, but got no responses. I phoned, but as soon as they knew it was me, the call was ended. I even went to the house one weekend, but again, the door was slammed in my face. I moved after that, as I couldn't bear being in the same neighbourhood and constantly worrying that I might bump into them or worse, see Michael and not be able to give him a hug. It was torture.

There was silence between us, as Michael processed all that I had said; his eyes never leaving my face, as though he was searching for answers; for the truth.

Eventually he said, "I love you Nan and I want you back in my life. Whatever went on, it was a long time ago and now we need to make more memories, happy ones. Agreed?"

"Agreed," I said, my heart so full of love and pure joy at getting a second chance to be a part of Michael's life and he to be a part of mine.

Chris Waterson

Common Ground

Poppy twisted the bobble twice and pulled at her hair until the ponytail felt secure. She had been quiet since entering the changing room as she prepared for their second lesson playing football.   They had all had a lot to say last week; "You're bound to be good, Poppy with your dad being a manager of a Premier League team." "Bet he's been giving you tips." "Some people have all the advantages- I'd love to play professionally in the future but my dad isn't even around." And the comments went on. The truth was that Poppy didn't like playing football. She may be a footballer's daughter but she did not have his talent. Kyle, her brother had got all of that.

"OK, Poppy, I'd like you to play centre forward today," instructed Ms Dixon. Poppy groaned inwardly; no chance of hiding away with that one. The game was tame for the first twenty minutes with the ball being at the other end of the pitch most of the time. She started to relax when she heard "Poppy, go for it!" as the ball flew through the air in her direction. She trapped the ball and then swiftly dribbled it up the pitch. Poppy was aware of the other team closing in on her but a clear run and an open goal, with a timid goalkeeper, was in sight. Realising that this was her chance to shine, she felt the adrenalin coursing through her and the butterflies dancing on her stomach. She kicked hard at the ball, aiming it at the wide goal mouth but the ball hit the side of her foot and it landed outside the post. Holding her head down in her hands, she heard the groans and exclamations of her team mates. Ms Dixon blew the whistle and walked over to her.

"Poppy, that was disgraceful. You had the perfect opportunity to score. What were you thinking of? I expect better than that. I don't know what your father would say."

Poppy took the criticism quietly but her cheeks were burning with humiliation. After the game, she showered quickly, kept her head down and left before too much could be said.

On her way home, she could hear a group of girls behind her talking about her and laughing. "Not any better than the rest of us are you?" one shouted and "Hey, two left feet."

Kyle was already home when she arrived and he was looking at his phone. "Do you deliberately try to embarrass me?" he asked. "Everyone is laughing at your pathetic attempts at football. It would be nice to have a sister who is cool for once," and he walked off.

All the criticisms of the day settled on her like a million wasp stings; she felt dejected and alone. The world did not love or understand her. In that moment, Poppy knew what she was going to do. Minutes later, she had a bag packed. On her way out, she borrowed the spare credit card that was only used when 'needs must' and added it to her £50 savings. She had no idea where she was going but Poppy did know that she had to go. After catching a bus into town, wandering around the shops until most of them closed, eating a burger in McDonalds, she was unsure what to do next. The train station might give her some inspiration, so she started off in that direction. On her way there she passed the community centre. The doors were open and there was a buzz of noise coming from inside. Poppy walked up the few steps and peered her head into the main hall. There was a crowd of people of various ages. Some were holding musical instruments.

"Come in. Join us," a relatively young man with straggly hair and a short beard called out to her. "Instrument or voice?"

"No. I was just curious. I haven't got an instrument."

"Voice then. Over there."

A slightly older woman approached her. "It's OK, love. The choir is over there, if you are interested. I know that it is a bit daunting but you will soon feel at home."

Poppy didn't know whether it was those words "feel at home" or because she didn't know what else she would do, she decided to stay. To her surprise, she enjoyed it. The first half of the evening was given over to explaining the purpose of the community choir and getting the instruments tuned up. This gave a lot of time for the others to chat quietly among themselves. Although the women on either side of her were much older than her, they were friendly and included her in their conversations. Poppy also noticed a few others who were closer to her age. After their refreshment break, Ted, (the man she had met originally) arranged them into soprano, alto, tenor and bass. Poppy was to sing soprano and they tried singing a few popular songs after some warm- up exercises. Poppy was surprised to find that it was already 9.45 when they finished.

"See you next week, Poppy," one of the women shouted after her.

"Yes. Fine."

Walking along the street at that time of night, now that the nights had drawn in, was not so fine. She felt all her senses on alert and became aware of a car that was kerb crawling her. She kept her eyes fixed ahead, so as not to encourage them and then she heard "Poppy, get in the car."

"Dad! What are you doing here?"

"I could ask you the same thing. Now get in. Your mother and I have been frantic with worry." They travelled home in silence.

Poppy braced herself for her mother's onslaught as she walked into the hallway but, for the third time that evening was surprised as she was greeted with a warm hug. "We have obviously been very worried and this cannot happen again but it isn't like you Poppy. Sit down. Have you eaten? Do you want to talk about what is going on?"

Over bacon sandwiches and a hot drink, Poppy described her day. "Well, I don't think the teacher should have said that. If someone is poor at maths and their father is an accountant, do they bring that up? I think we need to talk to the school," declared Mags indignantly.

"No, Mum. It will just make it worse."

"Well, I am definitely having a word with Kyle. I thought he looked sheepish. It was good that you only got involved in an innocent sing- a-long. It could have been a lot worse."

"I'd like to go back next week. It was fun."

Poppy's mother screwed up her face but her Dad jumped in.

"What's good about it, Poppy?"

"It's new, so everyone is equal-ish. The idea is that we compete with other community choirs and the winner gets to sing with a proper orchestra in London. It's like what that guy called Gareth did on TV."

"That sounds good. Why doesn't your mother go with you next week?" Poppy screwed *her* face up this time. "And find out about the people running it and what it entails. If she is happy, you can stay and if she has any doubts, you will leave without fuss."

Poppy wasn't totally enamoured with her dad's suggestion but knew that in the circumstances, it was probably the best that she could do.

The next rehearsal came round quickly and, after asking questions about safeguarding and other practicalities, Mags left informing Poppy that she would pick her up when it had finished.

For the next few months, the family fell into a routine. Dad, Kyle and Poppy had rehearsals at some time during the week and all had competitions on a Saturday; Dad was occupied with the Premier League, Kyle with the school football team and

Poppy with her choir. Saturday evening meal became the forum for feedback.

"Do you realise that Poppy is the only one who has come home every Saturday after having won?" pointed out Dad.

"Well, that's 'cos singing is easier than football," retorted an indignant Kyle.

"How would you know?" snapped Poppy.

"OK. That's enough. Show respect, Kyle for someone else's skills. That is an important quality of a sportsman."

The choir continued to outperform their competitors culminating in the Saturday when Poppy burst through the front door shouting out to the rest of the family "We won!! We won the final."

"That's fantastic, love."

"We are going to the Royal Albert Hall in three weeks' time and will be singing with the London Philharmonic Orchestra. And," she paused. "I am going to sing a solo."

Her parents exchanged looks of concern. "Are you sure that is what you want? I mean, it will be in front of a lot of people and remember the football…" Her mother got no further as she felt the well-practised kick of a footballer on her shin.

"That's very good. Why do you think they picked you?" asked her dad

"I've sung on my own before in rehearsals. They say that I have a lovely voice and it's powerful."

"They are right about that last bit," muttered Kyle.

"It's only a short solo – the first verse of *In the Bleak Mid-Winter*. It's part of the Carol Section."

For the next three weeks, Poppy took herself into the garage, practised scales and some of the pieces that the choir were going to sing in London. She also acquired three tickets for her parents and brother.

"You will be there, won't you Dad?" Poppy asked the night before the trip to London.

"Yes," he replied with his fingers crossed. "We kick off at Anfield at 12.00, so I should just make it."

Mick used all his charm on the usher to convince her to let him stand at the back of the auditorium even though the performance had started. Balancing family commitments and his work had been a constant struggle but he was determined to hear his only daughter, Poppy, sing. This was her Wembley. At the interval, he joined Mags and Kyle. Settled in his seat, the lights dimmed and the choir and orchestra took their places. Poppy's solo was the third item on the programme. He enjoyed the first two pieces, particularly noting what a good sound the amateur choir and professional orchestra made and how happy his daughter looked.

"Our next piece is *In the Bleak Mid-Winter* with first verse sung by Poppy Watkins."

Poppy stepped forward and stood behind the microphone. Mick felt his stomach knot and acknowledged that this was worse than any penalty shoot-out. *Keep in the zone, love*, he willed her. She opened her mouth and then it happened; the auditorium was filled with a sweet, clean and powerful melody. Her delivery was skilful; breathing was controlled to accentuate the phrasing, the pitch was perfect, her diction was clear, her poise confident and her being full of courage. Mick felt his eyes fill up and Mags squeezed his hand. Within minutes it was over. Poppy stepped back to her place. Her face was beaming with the joy of success.

"I am so proud of her," Mags whispered.

"She's got it, Mags. She really has. It's just not with a football."

Christine McCluskey

Sporting Rap

(In the manner of Stormzy, this rap is brought to you by Light Drizzly)

Sport can be fabulous, sport can be great
A bit like Marmite – you either love or you hate
Sport has energy coming to the fore
Sport is played instead of fighting war
This is the rap, the sporting rap

Cricketers do battle with bat and ball
Run a quick single is often the call
Two arms in the air and you've scored a six
A raised finger means out, so hit the bricks
In the rap, the Summer sports rap

Tennis at Wimbledon is really classy
But if it rains there's slippery grass(y)
Twenty quid buys strawberries and cream
The price of Pimm's is quite obscene
At the rap, the Summer sports rap

Football comes along when nights draw in
The roar of the crowd has quite a din
Rugby players chase after egg shaped balls
It's hard to tell the difference between rucks and mauls
So do the rap, the Winter sports rap

Sledging and Luge go quickly down hill
Wrap up warm to prevent catching a chill
Slalom skiers weave in and out
Then come crashing down, of that there's no doubt
With the rap, the Winter sports rap

Now fellow rappers it's time to leave
Let's go out jogging, it's fun I believe
Just watching sport can drive you crazy
So, participate – and don't be lazy
This was the rap, the sporting rap

Glance Puppy Pup
(Snoop Doggy Dog's apprentice)

Timothy Webb

Yoga for Beginners

I hadn't wanted to go to yoga classes. I wanted to join the art group, but it had been cancelled due to the teacher going on her maternity leave. Subsequently, yoga was the only session at the community centre which fitted in with my shifts. Steve, my ex had agreed to watch the kids for the couple of hours I'd be out, including getting there and back.

"Well, they are your kids too!" I reminded him.

I borrowed a DVD from my sister, which was supposed to show you what to do, as I didn't want to make an absolute fool of myself, and also a leotardy thing, which was, naturally, now too big for her! She went to an advanced group in town on Saturday mornings, not something I could manage in a month of Sundays, or indeed, Saturdays, as my Saturdays consisted of Leo's football practice, Stephanie's gymnastics, visiting my parents and trying to wrestle the house into some kind of hygienic order. The one brief oasis of inactivity was having a takeaway delivered.

I was late for the first session as I stopped to help an elderly lady who had almost tripped over a crack in the pavement. She was quite shaken up by it, so we sat on a handy low wall for a bit until she felt better.

"Yoga, eh?" she chuckled. "I always think of Yogi Bear and his pickernick baskets!"

"As you haven't brought a mat, you may borrow one of mine, but if you plan to continue with us then please bring your own."

My first encounter with Lucinda, the teacher, was less of a welcome and more of a ticking off; not the perfect start to achieving inner calm! I counted ten other women in the hall, all of whom seemed to be regulars and made for their habitual space on the floor. When I unfurled Lucinda's mat, a false fingernail fell out, giving me, not so much a shock, as the creeps. It was painted a lurid green, with sparkly bits on the tip. While I was trying to decide whether to pick it up or pretend I hadn't seen it and just leave it on the floor, I noticed the fingernails of the woman closest to me. They were all painted the same shade of green, with a similar embellishment. I then picked up the nail and offered it to her.

"Oh wow, thank you. I didn't know where it'd gone. Just hoping it hadn't fallen into anyone's food! That's what my boyfriend said, anyway." She made a loud snorting noise when she laughed, which, at first, I found endearing, but less so as the hour progressed. The other rather strange feature of her was her toenails. These were as far from pedicured, as her fingernails were manicured. They were really quite long and not very clean. As the lesson progressed, warm ups and stretches which I was able to join in with, I couldn't help looking at her feet. "I really want to supple up my legs. I've got a bet with my boyfriend that I'll be able to bite my own toenails within a month."

"Oh," I said, "that's why you've let them grow so long. But aren't they uncomfortable in your shoes?"

"Problem solved," she snorted and showed me her open toed sandals.

"Too much chatting at the back if you want to learn anything!" said Lucinda, quite sternly.

"Beam me up, Yogi," I thought.

We had a fifteen-minute loo/fag break halfway through the session, by which time, though, I had managed a Mountain pose and a Resting pose to Lucinda's satisfaction. They just seemed to me like standing up and lying down, but were obviously more 'Zen'. I went outside for a breather and found someone crying. Her name was Chloe and she told me she'd only come to the class tonight to get away from her ex-wife's voice. Apparently, she and her civil partner had split up, but were still living together as neither of them could presently afford to move to somewhere else.

"It's really getting us both down," said Chloe. "I used to love listening to her chat, and now it just gets on my nerves. Strange, isn't it, how love can just turn sour. Unless it wasn't really love anyway."

I commiserated with her, but my thoughts went to my own relationship with Steve. We'd been in love, hadn't we? We'd been happy together for over ten years, hadn't we? I'd told him to leave as I'd heard, from a reliable source, that he'd been seen out with another woman. He denied it, but he left, probably sick of the sight and sound of my accusations and snot filled howling. The children missed him terribly. I missed him. Was it worth giving it another chance? I thought this to myself, but found myself saying it aloud to Chloe. She gave me a quizzical look and then a smile, and we went back inside.

I got home by ten o'clock and Steve was actually still awake. The children were in bed and the house was quite tidy.

"How was it?" he asked. "Did you enjoy it? Were there any goats?"

"It was interesting," I said, trying not to laugh. "As much for the mix of women as the actual exercises. I'll go again. I mean I really want to master the Downward Dog."

"If I can help in any way with that manoeuvre," said Steve, with a familiar glint in his eye, "you have only to ask."

I bought a mat and continued with the sessions. Steve's babysitting duties turned into overnight stays. We both think it's definitely worth giving it another chance. As it happened, the art classes were re-opened with a new teacher, though they were on Saturday morning.

"Go," said Steve. I know you've always wanted to. I'll do the Saturday runs."

So, you see, not only do I get to study Yoga. I also get to study Goya!

Loraine Rutherford

Theatre of War

He stood in the broken doorway of his shattered home. His town had been devastated by rockets, tanks, and gunfire. Borysko, known to everyone as Borys, smoked a cigarette and thought longingly of his family. His wife, Anastasiya, and their daughter, Nataliya, had gone to live with Borys's brother Danylo when the fighting got uncomfortably close to their town. Danylo had moved to Germany for work a few years previously. He'd worked hard there and done well for himself, buying a house on the outskirts of Munich. Borys knew his family was safe there, but he missed them both dreadfully.

The evening was becoming dark, and Borys thought he could see a faint light up ahead... shimmering in the distance. He stood watching as the light seemed to come nearer, disappearing and reappearing. Stubbing out his cigarette, he edged silently towards the light, gun in hand.

After a few hundred yards Borys heard a strangulated shout and the light was extinguished. He edged forward cautiously. It could be a trap, but Borys was familiar with the enemy's tactics, and felt relatively safe. As he progressed forward, Borys heard a snuffling sound. It seemed to be coming from the ditch at the edge of the roadside. The light had completely vanished. Borys followed the ditch and in the dim light from his own torch he thought he saw a dark figure huddled in the bottom of the ditch. As he grew nearer it seemed to shrink down... trying to become part of the vegetation. Borys aimed his torch and gun at the figure, demanding, "Come out... hands above your head!" The figure hunched even lower and now Borys heard muffled sobbing.

He strode towards the figure, which hadn't moved but was shaking violently. As he reached the figure, gun outstretched, he saw it was a young Russian soldier... unarmed, it appeared. Borys grabbed him and yanked him up out of the ditch. He was shaking and begging for his life.

Now, Borys was on record as being a pacifist. He hated confrontation and any sort of physical violence. He'd only reluctantly taken up arms when his beloved country had come under threat, but he'd yet to kill anyone, and he didn't think now was the time to start.

Borys tried to calm the young lad... he looked about twelve, but obviously was older. It turned out he was a conscript who'd been sent to the front with no training. His name was Dimitri and he'd got left behind when his company had turned back. He hadn't wanted to be a soldier, but it was mandatory to serve two years. He was terrified they'd shoot him as a deserter.

Borys led him back to his house, gave him clothes, and together they burned his uniform.

Not everything is horror and death in the theatre of war. Compassion and kindness can be found in the most unlikely places.

Diane Gough

Memories of Yesterday

Do you remember those far off days
When we were so young and free?
The days seemed so long and
We would watch in childhood's innocence
The seasons rolling round.

Spring would come with flowers
And birdsong, the cuckoos in the wood,
Summer meant the seaside, playing in the sand
With buckets and spades.

Autumn meant the start of school, the leaves
Turning from green to red and brown.
Winter meant Christmas carols,
The school play and children's party.

I remember the old school in the village,
The small classrooms and the 'privie' down the yard.
The lane as it was, with the hedgerow and
Railway line, the crossing and the keeper.

As I think back, I see the faces I knew,
My classmates of long ago,
Where they are now, I don't know
Nor where life has taken them.

Time has slipped by and I no longer

Know some of the places I knew as
A child.

Kathleen Little

Little Miss Muffett

I'm big for my age. The ladies tell me I will be quite a catch but so far, I have been able to maintain a safe distance. They just love my tufty black hair and describe my large eyes as black pools of infinite depth. All in all, life is pretty good.

I've been lucky to find a very suitable place to set up home. There are wide open spaces all round and a convenient tuffet. It is very popular in the neighbourhood and has proved to be a very popular place for all manner of things to pop in for lunch, mine not theirs, so I am rather protective of my space.

I was just hanging out surfing the web to see if there are any interesting titbits for me to enjoy when I see the Muffett girl approaching. There she is skipping along, her yellow ringlets bobbing rhythmically beside her, her gingham summer dress floating along with her. I will need to keep a close eye or two on her. She could easily break my connection to the web and it will take me hours to reconnect. What is she carrying? A bowl, with a spoon sticking out of it. Why is she bringing food into the garden?

She is getting closer. Where is she going? Oh no, she is aiming for my tuffet. She's sitting on my tuffet. Thank you so much Miss Muffett, bang goes lunch. Nothing will come close with her sitting there. What on earth is that in her bowl? It looks decidedly unappetising. She seems to be enjoying it. Spoonful after spoonful she shovels, whatever it is, into her mouth. Between mouthfuls she is making the most extraordinary sounds. It could be music. Oh no, now she has started waving that spoon about. Watch it! She almost hit the web that time.

It's no good, I've got to do something. Any minute she will move too quickly, and the web will be lost. What to do? I know, I'll lower myself on to her shoulder and tickle her ear. That should persuade her to leave. Right, slowly down, adjusting for the wind, and a safe landing. Now, Tickle, tickle.

Now I will readily admit that when I thought up my plan of how I would succeed in persuading Little Miss Muffett to leave my tuffet I failed to fully consider all the possible consequences. Yes, when she felt me tickling her ear she did react. Yes, she did jump up and scream. Yes, she did destroy my web much as I had anticipated, but too late I realised the mistake of choosing to land on the right shoulder of a left-handed person.

With one swift and athletic move she drew the spoon from the bowl and brought it down smartly on her shoulder, the shoulder upon which I had landed. The last thing I, remember was seeing something very shiny approaching very quickly.

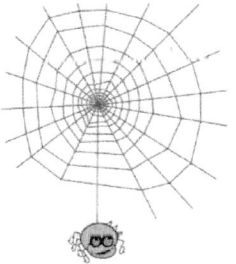

David Swinton

I Should Sphynx So

"How? I don't understand. How is this possible? I would not have believed it if I hadn't seen with my own eyes. John, once we end this call you have to get on a flight and come out here. The press teams are having a field day. I really am standing by the Sphynx – THE Sphynx for Christ's sake – and it's shrunk to the size of a domestic cat. My inner voice is screaming THIS IS IMPOSSIBLE yet here it is John, right in front of me, tiny. Some of the local journalists think it's linked to a strange light display in the sky last night but I don't believe them John. What do I think? In my professional opinion, using my years of experience, I firmly conclude it's some kind of Egyptian Government conspiracy to make the rest of the World look stupid. It can't be a coincidence that today marks the start of the Year of the Cat and the sandstorm John, the worst there's ever been apparently. The whole sky for miles in all directions was just full of orange sand. Hours it lasted, all week before this morning. The only thing that could be seen was those piercing bright lights, three retina burning points of red, black and white. They didn't seem to signify anything – they were just there.

    I've tried to send you pictures John, but the cameras just don't work. People have been trying to post on the internet, yet every image seems to autodelete. It's as though some evil Wizard has put a hex on the whole area. There's a village nearby and the residents have a prophesy that this would happen. Apparently, in their folklore, it occurred once previously many generations ago and is supposed to repeat itself after two thousand years or so. It sounds fantastical John, I know, yet here it is right in front of me. The Sphynx still even has the inscrutable smile, just in miniature. We must be careful how we release this John, as the information could lead to global panic, the kind not seen since Sydney Opera House developed those little round nobbles on top of every tile on its roof.

Wait a minute John something's happening. The points of light are back – red, white and black. They seem to be forming into some kind of a sign in the air, just like Batman used to have in those comic books. Yes John, it's settling now. I don't know what it means. It's just a single word – LEGO."

Timothy Webb

Polly and Sukey

>Polly put the kettle on,
>Polly put the kettle on,
>Polly put the kettle on,
>We'll all have tea.
>
>Sukey take it off again,
>Sukey take it off again,
>Sukey take it off again,
>They've all gone away.

"It's switched on. So, in your own time ...."

Mabel sighed. "Well at first it was very endearing. They are twins, you know and when they were young, they would play dollies tea parties. Just like the nursery rhyme, Polly would put the kettle on and the dolls would sip their tea. Then Sukey would take the kettle off and the dolls would be put away. The adults even sang the nursery rhyme sometimes when they were playing. Both the girls loved it."

"They were happy times for you?"

"Yes, definitely. They were beautiful little girls."

"Did they always get on well when they were growing up?"

"Mostly, yes. There was one occasion. They would be five, I think. They hadn't been at school long. Polly brought home a painting. She had been given a gold star for it. It was very good, so we put it on the fridge door. I thought the girls were playing quietly together until Polly came to me sobbing and dragged me into the kitchen. Sukey had taken the painting off the fridge and had coloured over it in bright red. She got a good telling off. It disturbed me, that incident. Tom and I wondered if Sukey felt second best, as she was the younger of the two by 30 minutes, and that we needed to give her some individual attention. My mum warned me to stamp out that kind of behaviour before it got out of hand. I am happy to say, however, that we had years of normal sibling interaction after that.

It wasn't until they were sixteen that there was another incident. Polly had a lovely boyfriend, Darren and all three of them were friends. We had a joint birthday party for the girls. They both looked lovely (and very grown up, I remember thinking). Tom and I were there but tried to keep a low profile. All seemed to be going well but, to cut the story short, Polly caught Sukey flirting with Darren and making herself irresistible. I was disappointed in Darren, as well as Sukey. They started seeing each other but she only played him along for a few weeks and then dumped him. Polly and Sukey didn't speak to each other for weeks. It was a hard time consoling Polly and trying to get Sukey to understand what she had done. We also needed to understand why she had hurt her sister in that way."

"Did you get an answer?"

"Not really. Sukey thought it was normal teenager behaviour; what her friends did. She didn't use these words but it was almost "All's fair in love and war." I was very disappointed. I thought that we had done a better job at bringing them up than that. In some ways we had because the following years were filled with success for both of them; they both achieved good degrees and would socialise with each other. They were not only sisters, but the best of friends. I thought that both of them had finally grown up." Mabel stopped and looked down. Eventually she resumed.

"We were so delighted when Sukey announced that she was getting married to Rich. Polly was her chief bridesmaid and they had great fun organising the wedding. Polly never showed any jealousy. It was another four years before Polly got married to Dave and a big surprise for everyone when she became pregnant so quickly. Looking back, I remember feeling a little concerned. It wasn't common knowledge but Sukey had confided in me that they had been trying for a baby for well over a year. I hoped that she could be happy for her sister and it seemed that she was. She was supportive and interested in Polly's pregnancy and when the baby was born doted on her. Polly and Sukey could often be seen pushing the pram through the park together. There was that synchronicity between them that they had when they were young. Sukey bonded well with little Emily. That is why …" Mabel paused.

"Would you like to take a break?"

"Just give me a few moments." Mabel sat twisting her handkerchief around her fingers. "It was a sunny day and I received a phone call from Polly. She was hysterical. Emily had gone missing. She had left her for a moment in her buggy in the back garden while she used the bathroom. On her way back to Emily her phone had rung which she had left on the kitchen table. She made a quick detour to pick it up and then went out to Emily to find that there was nothing other than an empty buggy. It can't have been more than 4 or 5 minutes that she left her. Polly will live with that for the rest of her life. From that moment on everything was chaos; police, searches, questions. I'll never forget the look of torment in Polly and Daves' eyes. We all did what we could. Sukey and Rich went out on all the searches day and night and Tom and I tried to support the others as well as we could. All the days rolled into one as we waited for news. First, we hoped for good news but then it slowly waned day by day.

On day four, the police called at the house. A neighbour, who had just returned from being away for a few days, had reported seeing a red car leaving from Polly's house at the time that Emily was taken. I was then asked the worst question of my life. 'Did I know anyone with a red car?' Well, I did because Sukey's car was red. They had to ask me three times because I didn't know how to reply. I have two daughters, you see and I wanted to protect both of them. You are probably wondering why I felt the need to protect Sukey and it was because the moment that they asked the question something that I had unconsciously known suddenly became known to me. In the end, I told them that Sukey had a red car because logic also tells me that thousands of people have red cars. That set the ball rolling.

Sukey was taken in for questioning and the house was searched. Another piece of my heart broke when Rich, a hunk of a man, sat in front of me crying like a baby over the accusations that were being levied at Sukey. Sukey denied all of it; in fact, was outraged that they could suspect a doting aunt of taking her niece. Polly believed in Sukey's innocence."

"Was it long after that that Emily was found?"

"A week, maybe ten days. You will know the details from the news that a family, on a day out at Brimham Rocks, found her."

"Did Brimham Rocks have any meaning for you?

"Yes. It was a place where we used to take the children for a play and a picnic. In fact." Mabel suddenly stopped.

"Are you alright?"

"I have just remembered something. I don't know why I haven't recalled it before. On one occasion, the girls took a doll each. Polly realised halfway home that she had left hers behind. We tried to console her by promising that we would buy her a new one, but she would not be placated and, in the end, we had to turn round and find dolly. It was Sukey who found her between two large boulders."

"Like Emily?"

Mabel nodded. Eventually, she resumed. "The police made a search of the area and watched the CCTV footage at the car park. There was a clear recording of Sukey carrying Emily. From then on, we walked into our own hell; the grief of the confirmed death of Emily, the utter devastation of a sister betraying her twin and the guilt of being failed parents. I have never felt such torment." Mabel looked at her hands in her lap. The silence and sorrow hung in the room like a damp mist. She looked up. "I had to do this interview. For the money, so we can move. You see, Sukey took Emily off and the rest of us have to go away."

Christine McCluskey

The Mystery at the Castle

Not much of the castle is still standing; its walls have crumbled and its once majestic turrets no longer exist.

As Ruth gazes at what is left of the ruin and its sad reflection in the water, she imagines what it looked like when it was a fortress, repelling marauders; a stately home entertaining nobility; a revered landmark of historical interest. How had such grandeur been reduced to rubble? Neglect and Mother Nature's fiercest elements had no doubt brought about its demise, being well beyond restoration.

Ruth settles herself on a grassy bank at the edge of the lake and takes out her sketch pad and pencils from her rucksack. It's pleasantly warm, but not overly sunny, which suits her mood to draw the remains of the castle, surrounded by tall trees and mirrored in the lake against a background of grey sky.

It doesn't take her long to produce a good outline for her picture and she's keen to apply colour to bring it to life. She only has crayons, but quickly captures the tints of the bricks, foliage and water.

Feeling hungry and wishing she'd bought a picnic and not just a flask of coffee and snack bar, Ruth pauses to take refreshment and idly photographs the scene on her mobile phone. This will help her remember the ambience when she transfers her sketch onto canvas.

Her thoughts wander again, daydreaming about how the castle must have looked centuries ago. A very slight movement in the lake takes her attention and she automatically points her phone and presses the button a couple of times, but when she looks to see what it could be, there's just a few ripples. Something like a fish or an otter must have surfaced and disappeared again, she thinks to herself.

She hears humming, but can't see any bees nor, she now notices, is there any bird song except for the occasional caw of a crow. The wind is getting up; shrilly whistling through sturdy branches, the late summer leaves clinging obstinately, as small waves lap the shingle below where she's sitting.

Involuntarily, Ruth shivers and gathers up her belongings, hastily putting them in her rucksack before hoisting it on to her back and scrambling uphill to the footpath and hurrying to her car.

Once inside, she takes a deep breath to steady herself, not sure why she feels so afraid.

"Get a grip," she tells herself sternly and then with a chuckle, "this place certainly has atmosphere!"

She starts the car and carefully drives along the unmade track, relieved when she reaches the road that will take her back to civilisation.

Ruth is on holiday and staying in a charming little cottage, conveniently situated next to a pub. Most evenings she's taken advantage of the home-cooked meals on offer and tonight is no exception.

The landlord greets her cheerily, "What have you been up to today?"

"I went to the ruined castle to sketch," she replied and produced the little image for him to see. "I'm going to put it on canvas when I get home."

"Impressive," the landlord says admiringly, "you've captured the place well."

Ruth takes out her phone to show him the photos she's taken and hands it to him.

"You weren't alone then," he says swiping through the pictures curiously.

Ruth looks puzzled and peers at the screen. To her amazement, there's a cloaked and hooded figure emerging from the woods and another kneeling at the water's edge, looking into the lake.

"They weren't there," she says aghast, "I'd have seen them."

A shiver crawls up her spine, as she takes the phone to look at the pictures she took of the lake. Unbelievably, there's something visible in the water; it looks like a hand holding a large dagger. She hands the phone back to the landlord, "Do you see what I see?" she asks shakily.

The landlord stares at the screen, enlarging the picture to take a closer look. Frowning he says, "The sword of Damocles," then mutters, "I've heard stories, but never believed them. Are you sure you didn't see anything?"

"Nothing," Ruth says adamantly, "but I heard humming and then the wind got up; it was very spooky."

"They say the place is haunted and that's why the locals tend to avoid it; I thought it was all poppycock, but this is proof beyond belief!"

Ruth looks at her phone as though it might explode; fright etched all over her face. The landlord pours them both a large brandy and patting her hand says, "It's weird, but it won't hurt you."

"It's definitely very weird and no wonder I was terrified." Sipping her brandy, Ruth dared to look again at the photographs. All she sees now are the images she thought she'd recorded; the castle ruins and the woods, reflected in the ripples on the lake. No hooded figures or sword of Damocles. She stares in disbelief, her mouth open, but no words come. She passes the phone to the landlord, who seeing the look on her face, scrutinises the photos again. He too, sees nothing but the ruins and the lake.

"That's unbelievable," he says aghast, "we can't both have seen something so unreal; we can't both have imagined it!"

"We must have," Ruth says hopefully, rather than convinced and doubting any kind of explanation. She swipes away from the photos and taps back in again. The images of the castle and lake are exactly how she captured them; not a hooded figure or sword anywhere in sight. She powers off her mobile, leaves it a few minutes and switches it on again. The photos are all perfectly normal, no mysterious images visible.

"Well, no one's going to believe us, so there's not much point in saying anything to anyone," the landlord says philosophically.

"We can't prove anything – people will think we're mad!" Ruth agrees.

"We know what we saw and it looked real didn't it?"

"It did, but clearly it wasn't! Maybe I should delete the photos and forget all about them."

"If you can, which I doubt, so maybe visit the castle again?"

"Absolutely no way!" Ruth declares.

So, the history and the mystery remain.

Chris Waterson

The Staircase

I didn't trip down the stairs. He came up behind me and I felt the shove as he pushed me. I remember the ground coming up to meet me, the stone floor as unforgiving as the demons in Hell. I hope that's where he went, when his time came.

He spread the story that I had tripped and because he was the master of the house, the Police believed him. I was just a silly servant girl who had fallen pregnant. He always pretended it had been another servant who had put a baby in me. It was him, nobody else, and when the doctor said I would have a baby and I went to tell him, he told me to leave. I was fired.

He followed me to the staircase, then one shove and I was gone.

Every year, on that anniversary, I return to that staircase, re-enacting my fall, for anyone who can see those of us who are no longer your side of the living. One day, I hope, someone will work it out and I will be reunited with my unborn little one.

Please see me, a seventeen-year-old servant girl, on that staircase. Just say, "I see you" and I shall be free.

Emma Eyers

The Owl

Two Hoots the Tawny owl lived in a wood near a village. He would often sit in his favourite tree near the village church and watch the comings and goings of the villagers. One day he saw a lot of activity in the church grounds, some people were putting flowers around the church lych gate, others were carrying flowers into the church. When they had all left, he flew down from his tree to investigate.

He didn't get very far as more people arrived, so he flew back into his tree and watched from the safety of his favourite tree branch. The people went into the church, and after a while came back out again. Two Hoots curiosity was heightened when he saw the vicar come out of the church with a young couple and said that all was ready and he would see them tomorrow morning.

Two Hoots flew down to one of the windows and tried to peep in, but he couldn't see because the stained glass didn't allow him to see inside. He would have to wait until tomorrow to find out what was happening and where the flowers were. That night Two Hoots couldn't sleep, he kept thinking about what he'd seen and was determined to find out.

The following day Two Hoots watched as cars started arriving, lots of people got out of them and walked through the lych gate, down the path and into the church. The young man Two Hoots had seen the day before was among them, with another young man who he hadn't seen before, both looking very smart in their suits. They too went through the lych gate, down the path and were met at the church door by the vicar, who they followed inside.

After a short while Two Hoots saw a very smart car arrive, decked with ribbons. The driver's door opened and a very smartly dressed man got out, went to the passenger door at the rear and helped out an older man, also very smartly dressed. Both men then went to the other passenger door and helped out the young lady that he'd seen the day before. She was wearing a very pretty white dress, with a long thing which Two Hoots had never seen before so didn't know what it was. She was carrying a bunch of yellow flowers, which he thought was very pretty. Another car arrived also decorated with ribbon, out of this car came an older woman and three young girls dressed in pretty dresses, the three girls also carried bunches of yellow flowers.

Two Hoots watched as the young lady, the older man walking alongside her and the girls, shepherded by the older woman, walked behind and carried the long thing as well as their flowers, went through the lych gate, down the path and into the church porch. Here they waited then moved forward into the church as Two Hoots heard music from within the church.

The church door had been left open, so he flew down to see if he could see inside. Very quietly he flew into the porch, settled on a perch and peeped through the door. Two Hoots had never seen inside the church before so he sat looking around and watched as the vicar took the service. He saw the older man give the young ladies hand to the vicar, who then gave her hand to the younger man. Two Hoots was confused by this. He then heard the younger man repeat promises after the vicar, then the young lady did the same. Two Hoots knew what promises were, his mum had promised him a nice fat juicy mouse when he was a little chick – and very nice it was too. He licked his beak remembering. Then the young man and young lady followed the vicar into a room at the back of the church that Two Hoots couldn't see into.

Soon the music started again and Two Hoots was noticed for the first time, as everyone watched the young man and young lady walk down the church and towards the door.

Two Hoots flew back through the porch and went and watched from the safety of his tree. Everyone assembled in the church yard and photos were taken. The couple pointed out Two Hoots to the person taking the photos, so one photo was taken of the young couple pointing to the tree where Two Hoots was sat.

Two Hoots didn't really understand what was happening or what all the fuss was about, but he felt very proud when he heard the older man who had walked down with the young lady earlier say to someone that the owl was a lucky omen and a very welcome wedding guest who would bring peace and happiness to the couple.

Kathleen Little

Groping in the Fog

One evening, I was walking from the theatre during the dark month of November. The air was quite nippy and a fog was descending quickly. Normally, I would not have ventured out, but tonight was the last showing of a film called 'Black Lady', which had had rave reviews, so I decided to make the effort.

I had left my car in a nearby car park, but the fog had descended so quickly, I could hardly see my hand in front of my face. I was wishing I had brought a torch with me as my phone was little better than useless to guide my way and, on top of that, there appeared to be what sounded like an older gentleman groping around in the fog, which looked and felt a little suspicious.

By now I was lost. I kept telling myself that I would see the nearby café or a sign that would guide me back to the car park. Through the murky blackness, I found the café and hoped that there would be someone in there who could direct me to where the Bower Street car park was situated.

I sat down at first, but realised I had to go to the counter to order my latte and ask for directions. Bower Street turned out to be a few hundred yards up the road.

Low and behold, the 'elderly' gentleman, who appeared to be following me, came over to my table. He said that he had heard my conversation and wondered if he could help. He looked friendly, nicely dressed and old enough to be my father. His name was Stanley and although I was at first suspicious, I felt myself warming to him. Stanley asked whereabouts I was travelling to, which turned out to be the next village to his, plus he was the father of a very close friend of mine and like me, had been to the theatre. After a minute or two, he looked around the café to see no one else was listening and admitted, in rather a quiet voice, that he was lost too, but too embarrassed to ask!

Who knows!

Betty Mitcheson

Tea on the Train

The Writer, having recently had almost terminal bloc, decided to take the subject to the source. Equipped with a cheese sandwich and a flask of tea, a train up the coast was sought out and duly boarded. Deep thought occurred. A recent reading group had proffered a stream of consciousness novel, so why not have a go at such a piece? No idea of plot and direction, just write.

After around an hour, the train arrived at a decaying seaside town. Buildings, once grand, were now rotting yet still standing and holding Charity Shops and Turkish Barbers with a particular focus on Tanning Salons and Nail Bars. Sandwiches, flask and notebook in hand, the Writer headed for the Seafront. After about a half hour of productive scribble, during which the Writer had got – well – about this far through a story, the rain began tumbling apace. Not wishing to risk newly coiffured hair and still tacky nails the Writer beat a hasty retreat to the nearest hostelry. A dozen wooden tables hosting two dozen wooden people greeted the newly entered guest, all of whom were no doubt dodging the showers. No spaces. In the far corner stood a single table, raised slightly up on a kind of ramp. It held one person. A peculiar looking lady with more crinkles than anything else, both on her overcoat and her face. She motioned at the Writer and pointed out a seat beside her yelling, "There's room here love." The rest of the room turned to see the response so the Writer, not wishing to seem rude, dutifully alighted at the proffered seat with a large degree of trepidation. A Waitress attired in a uniform smelling of mothballs swiftly appeared.

"What's your poison? We do a flight of three thirds of ale for a good price and the meat pies are going down a storm."

The Writer settled on three strong ales and an aforementioned pie with thrice cooked chips.

"And for your Companion?"

The Writer noticed for the first time the Companion did not have a drink in front of her so dutifully offered to provide one.

"Oh, thanks love, I'll have a large glass of house white and a packet of cheese and onion. Have to watch my weight you know," she cackled adjusting her coat.

"My name's Maisy and this is Harold," she pointed to her lap which contained a small retractable umbrella and a smaller retractable dog with floppy ears. The Writer presumed the dog, not the umbrella to be named Harold.

There then followed a couple of breathless unasked for minutes of life history which the Writer allowed to enter in one ear and leave from the other before the Waitress reappeared with the drinks.

A small commotion and a brief round of applause broke out at the other end of the bar. A shabby man whose overcoat was similar to the Companion's began playing an aging steel guitar and singing of some lost land blighted by potato famine. The lyrics inferred that despite all having emigrated to much better places everyone longed to return to this isle which apparently held the actual God as well as many things of beauty.

"If it's so good there they should never have left," asserted the Companion.

The Waitress reappeared with food.

"Any more drinks? You must be nearly ready by now."

The Companion swiftly drained the wine.

"Another large glass for me and bring another one of those flight things," she ventured. Searching briefly inside a large handbag she exclaimed, "Oh, seems I've left my purse at home. You don't mind buying do you love?" The Waitress didn't wait for an answer and rapidly disappeared to fetch the drinks.

"Must just pop to the loo," announced the Companion, loudly. "I'll tie Harold's lead to the chair, he'll be no bother." With that she struggled to her feet revealing leopard skin plastic trousers which not so much hugged every undulation as stuck themselves in place. They and the shabby coat waddled off towards the door on far too high pink battered heels.

The drinks arrived and the Writer swiftly ordered another flight of ale, having a feeling it might be necessary.

The meat pie was surprisingly tasty, although the meat was of uncertain origin and the chips only acceptable when covered in ketchup.

After several minutes the Companion reappeared, sporting freshened up lipstick, the coat now open, to reveal a crisp white top with buttons undone almost to the naval.

Across the room the Crooner started up another song about loss and loneliness. The Writer felt a hand alight on a leg but by now there was no caring. As the drinks took effect the afternoon became an increasing blur. This must be a Tuesday; the Writer could never get the hang of Tuesdays.

Timothy Webb

The Bus Shelter

I was invited to dinner for a housewarming party being given in the, new, five-bedroom detached house, by two old friends from university. I had been best man at their wedding. Sophy, as well as a good doctor, is an excellent cook and Graham is a wine connoisseur, so I decided not to drive to the party as it was impossible to imagine that I would be in a fit state to drive home after what was bound to be a very convivial evening

Shortly after midnight the party began to disperse. When told that I intended to catch the night bus, Graham immediately volunteered to drive me home. He was plainly in no state to be driving, which he eventually agreed, so he offered to call a taxi. I assured him that I was more than happy to use the night bus and following emotional farewells, I set off to find the bus stop.

After some twenty minutes, I reach the main road which I knew was on the bus route. Looking along the road, I could see a bus shelter and walked towards it. It was plainly a new shelter, there was no graffiti, and all the glass was in place. I checked the timetable and was pleased to see that I would only have to wait 12 minutes for the bus.

Since leaving Graham and Sophy's I had not seen another pedestrian and standing in the bus shelter looking at the bus approaching I could see no-one. When I turned to face the road where the bus would be stopping, I was surprised to find that I had been joined by an elderly couple, a young man and a young woman with a pram. I gave a general nod and a short "Hi" but received no acknowledgement. As the bus eased to a halt my phone rang. I turned my back to the bus to answer it but there was no indication of an incoming call. From behind me, I heard the driver shout, "Are you getting on, Mate?" Stepping onto the bus I apologised, but while the driver was issuing my ticket, I could not help noticing that there were no passengers. I asked the driver where the other passengers had gone and he replied, "What other passengers?"

"The old couple, the woman with a pram and a young lad", I said.

The driver shut the door, gave me a look that said, "You must have had a skinful," and we set off. I must have nodded off because the next thing I knew, the driver was giving me a nudge and saying, "This is your stop." Muttering a thank you, I left the bus and opened my front door.

Safely home, I went to bed and slept well. In the morning, I had happy memories of the party, but didn't think anything about the bus ride home.

Later in the week the local newspaper arrived. It is a free sheet and, frankly, I use it more for wrapping rubbish than a source of news. My eye was drawn to a paragraph on the front-page recounting that a bus driver had committed suicide the day he had been due in court on a charge for causing the death of five people, including a six-month-old baby, when he crashed into a bus shelter. I do not believe in ghosts, but something forced me to check more of the detail of the accident. It had happened on the very road and the very bus stop where I had caught the bus.

Then I saw the picture of the driver. My legs gave way, and I fell into a chair. Unless he had a twin, this was the man who had brought me home from the party. Worrying thoughts flooded into my mind. How had the driver known where I lived and why had he been driving down a road that is not on any bus route in a bus with no other passengers?

David Swinton

I'll Never Stop Saying...

It is the last photograph I have of her, and I'm quite proud of it. It captures that look of concentration on her young face, the set of her mouth, the focus in her eyes, pencil poised as she watches the mare and foal she wishes to commit to paper. I'd begun to take the camera with us when we went out, whether on walks like this one, or to the supermarket or the fair, whatever, as she'd watched an interview with some successful artist who described the taking of photographs as a useful tool for memorising an interesting scene or event, from which to then recreate it in a drawing or painting, adding to it by one's own technique and individuality. She had already taken some snaps of the horses, but, as they helpfully stayed by the fence, she decided to try to sketch them from life. I took only the one photo of her as I'd been admonished for spoiling her concentration. The man appeared above her in the field in which she was sitting. I expected a dog to follow him from somewhere, and would have been annoyed had it disturbed the horses. But there was no dog which was good, and as he was dressed for walking: sturdy shoes, backpack, binoculars, I answered his greeting of "Hello, beautiful day," with something similar to wish him on his way.

We're not supposed to have favourites among our children. We're damn lucky to have them when others can't. I'm not saying she was my favourite, but she was special. I'd had three boys; a single birth, Tom, then twin boys, James and Stephen, and wasn't intending to have any more children. It was the holiday in Tenerife, our first holiday together without the boys, good old mum, which produced our daughter, Maria, a golden child who fed, slept, smiled, rarely cried, played, grew, was never really ill, met all her milestones, liked and was successful at school, a budding artist, was kind, and was loved by all who knew her. Perhaps she was too good for this world.

Jones. His name was Frank Jones. I remember thinking what an ordinary name for someone who did such an extraordinary and appalling thing. I thought he'd gone off on his walk, but when I looked up he was walking, or rather, striding towards us, without his backpack and binoculars, but carrying something shiny in his hand.

"Hello again," I said.

He said nothing but lunged at me with the knife stabbing me in the stomach and shoulder. I yelled to Maria to run, but she was unclear as to what was happening and just stood, transfixed. He took her. My child. I never saw her alive again. I passed out with shock and blood loss, but when I came to, I rang the Police, and the nightmare, in which I still live, continued to unfold. I wanted her to be alive, of course I did, but I wished her dead to whatever he might do to her. They found her body four months later, at the same spot from which he took her. He told the Police he wanted her to be able to watch the horses. According to Jones, he hadn't intended to hurt her, but he'd squeezed her too tightly, to stop her from screaming and fighting him. She'd broken his nose, yet there were hardly any marks on her body, and no sign of sexual interference, which was a blessing for want of a better word.

Is there a suitable punishment for those who carry out such acts? I don't think so. Crying for vengeance is still crying and the whole family has done a lot of that. I've recovered physically but I wish I'd died with her, or better still, instead of her. Her father, Bill, struggles every day to put one foot in front of the other, to do ordinary things. We rely on the boys a lot and then wish we didn't as they've lost their sister and have their own grief and their own lives to manage. Our oldest, Tom and his wife, are expecting their first child, I wonder what that will do to us all? My mother sometimes forgets and asks about her granddaughter and then howls with the pain of the recollection.

I look at this photograph a lot. The Police recovered my camera 'at the scene' as they say, but we couldn't have it back for a while as it was evidence. They were able to take Jones's DNA from me and I was able to give them a good description of the monster who ripped our lives apart because he was 'lonely'. I keep his face as clearly in my memory as I can because his was the last face she would've seen, and I feel that I share those last moments with her. Three years ago now, Maria, my darling girl. In this photo you are still alive, like the mare and foal in your last sketch; still your vibrant self, full of so much potential. You are caught as in aspic, as in amber. Your name is always on our lips. And the world has dimmed without you, Maria.

Loraine Rutherford

The Final Act

"If you go, don't bother coming back!" Lesley screamed.

Jason slammed shut the door he'd been about to go through and turned, red-faced and angry, "I've had enough!" he roared.

Lesley looked startled; this was a different man to her normally submissive husband, who nearly always apologised for whatever had started the argument, even if it wasn't his fault.

Jason saw Lesley's expression change from haughty to confused and in that split second, realised he, for once, had the upper hand.

"I mean it," he yelled, "I've had enough!"

"But I love you, you know I do," wheedled Lesley, sidling towards him, her arms outstretched.

"You've got a bloody funny way of showing it!" Jason retorted, grabbing her hands before they went around his neck and pushed her away.

For years, he'd taken abuse, verbal and physical, which often left him feeling battered and bruised. Lesley could pick a fight about anything; Jason loathed confrontation and would try to diffuse the situation, mostly through conciliation, rather than have a row. Sometimes it worked, sometimes it didn't, but frequently he asked himself why he put up with it, why did he tolerate such humiliation?

Today, something snapped inside him and a red mist descended. He stared hard at his wife, still incredibly beautiful and elegant, but what he saw was a tormentor, unkind and ungrateful. He circled her, like a lion prowling before pouncing on its prey.

"You're scaring me, Jason, stop it at once," Lesley demanded, backing into a corner of the hallway.

Jason leaned over her, his hands reaching for the silk scarf tied around her neck; he pulled the ends, squeezing her throat; watched, as her eyes bulged and her face turned crimson. Such was his focus, he was unaware of a hand reaching for an ornament to strike him, the blow connecting with the side of his head.

Jason buckled; Lesley took her last gasp and landed on top of him.

A concerned neighbour, having heard the shouting, summoned Police when it suddenly went quiet.

Two lifeless bodies were taken to the morgue and post mortems carried out.

At the inquest, the Jury voted unanimously that both deaths were due to unnatural causes and unlawful, but that no other party was involved.

Chris Waterson

The Letter

The lady at number 48 Rosemary View was surprised to find a letter, addressed to her, being delivered through her door. She was elderly and couldn't remember the last time an actual letter had come through her door. Her address was right, but they had spelled her name a bit wrong. She figured it must be for her though, as it was the year 2024 and, in all seriousness, who still writes letters?

She lifted the envelope up, looking at the plain white envelope, seeing it as the pale blue envelope her first love had sent. She could see it all again now: her excitement at the anticipation of what that envelope so long ago might contain.

She hadn't been sheltered back then, oh no! She knew that when young lads gave those envelopes to girls, it would eventually lead to him asking for the girl's hand. Back then, she remembered, it would be confusing, as she didn't understand what "asking for her hand" meant. Why just her hand? Why not the rest of the girl?

She felt the white envelope, remembering how her dad had reacted to her first letter from a boy, her first love.

"You're too young to be courting," he had told her firmly, as he had taken the letter off her, throwing it, unopened and unread, into the flames.

The old lady shook her head, bringing her mind back to the present, knowing she couldn't dwell on the past. She had never been able to find out the contents of that letter and never would. She knew who it had been from, as her dad had told her mum it was "that boy again".

She slowly ran her finger along, opening the envelope, taking her time, so as to prolong the anticipation - which she hadn't been able to do back then, with that envelope.

She slid the paper out and slowly opened it, with her arthritic fingers. She slowly read the words to herself.

"I know you don't know me, but my grandpa always talked about you. It took several years for us to be able to find you. He never forgot you and always talked about you. I'll keep this short as I realise you probably moved on long ago and married someone else. He is in our local care home, as his needs now are more than we can give him.

His name is Gordon Banks and his address, if you want to see him again, is:

    Meadowbrook Care Home
    Fernside Hill
    Wishford
    Surrey

He married someone else, but when my grandma passed away, he went back to his original name, the one he grew up with. Please visit him, he would love to see you again. You were his first love and he never once forgot you.

From James.

The old lady hugged the letter and the envelope to her chest, and gazed out of the window, lost in the memories again of those far off years.

Emma Eyers

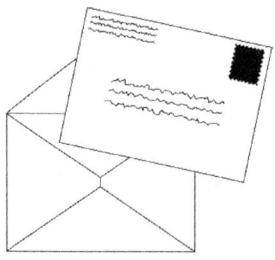

Ah Yes, I Was Expecting You

"Ah yes, I was expecting you. Come in and shut the door." Trying to remain calm I looked at this person who, I assumed, had been responsible for the death of three of my colleagues and had now come to continue the contract. Dressed in black from a ski mask, with only his eyes visible, to black trainers, he looked very fit and able to carry out the mission and there was an ugly pistol pointing at me.

The eyes never left me, neither did he speak as he walked slowly towards me. Fortunately, he could not see that my left knee was pressing the button under my desk. This sounded an alarm in the command post set up two days previously by the security services in response to the murders of my colleagues. The security officer had told me to keep him talking to give them time to respond to the alarm. What do you say to the man who intends to shoot you. Looking at the lack of expression in his eyes I doubted he was in the mood for a casual chat.

"I understand none of my former colleagues suffered and died instantly, for that I thank you, and hope that when the time comes, you will be equally merciful to me. I assume you have been contracted to carry out the executions of my team and myself and in a strange way I am grateful that you have left me to the last. I presume someone has simply given you a list of names and said they must be killed, but I do wonder if you have ever asked yourself why we deserve to die. I would be happy if you could explain the reason, but I honestly have no idea what we have done that demands such a dramatic response." I paused to see if there was any suggestion of him speaking, but plainly there was none.

I sat in silence pondering the fact that shortly I would be dead. I hoped I had left my affairs neat and tidy, my will simple and clear and that there wouldn't be too much of a mess for Mrs Watson, who comes in to clean on a Thursday, to clear up. I am a little concerned that it might be her who finds my body, if the security people don't respond to the alarm. I know it's silly, but I am also worried that my antique desk might be damaged; it could be worth a bob or two. Perhaps I should ask him to let me walk out into the garden and he could shoot me there.

I look at him again. Still no discernible expression in the eyes, but what would be the correct expression for an assassin who is about to carry out his mission. Looking again at my would-be executioner, I realised that he did seem to be rather small with a lightness of frame. Not the typical ex-army soldier I would have expected.

"I know I am shortly to die, and I am sure you believe that I deserve to die, but I can't help wishing I knew what I had done that deserves this end."

The right hand continued to hold the gun pointing straight at me, but the left hand rose above the shoulder and began to pull off the ski mask. For a moment I could not believe what I was looking at. Once the mask was removed long and lustrous black hair fell over her shoulder and down her back. She was, unquestionably, not a man but an attractive young woman. I looked at her closely but could not recognise her from anything in my past. Suddenly she spoke as if in answer to my internal questioning.

"Do not try to work out if you have ever seen me before. You have, but that was over twenty years ago and at that time, I was only seven years old and I suspect I have changed somewhat over the years."

I simply didn't know what to say and just sat there hoping she would say more.

She continued, "I was living with my grandfather after both my parents were killed by a bomb. On a dark wet night my grandfather and I were walking home. I had just crossed a road and stopped to see where my grandfather was. He was an old man and could walk only slowly. We both heard a car approaching quickly. He was unable to move fast enough, and the car hit him and tossed him on to the road. At first, I thought the driver had not realised what had happened, but the car came to a stop some distance along the road. Four men climbed out and went to look at the front of the car, I assume to see if there was any damage. With much laughter and general jollity three of the men climbed back into the car but one, the driver, looked up the street and could see something lying on the road. As he began to walk towards my grandfather, the three in the car called out for him to hurry up. He stopped and called back that he was just going to look to see what he had hit. Again, the men in the car shouted that he should hurry up and said it was probably just a stray dog or something. The driver paused, looked at my grandfather lying in the road, said they were probably right, walked back to the car and drove away. You were the driver of that car. By the time an ambulance arrived, my grandfather was dead. I managed to live in his house for some months before I fell into the hands of social services and became part of the care system. For the past 15 years, I have been establishing who were the men in the car that killed my grandfather. As you know I found all of you and you are the last."

I didn't know what to say in reply. I did remember the incident but not the outcome. Saying sorry would not be sufficient and, if I was honest with myself, I could fully understand her wish for revenge. Then, to my horror I noticed two little red dots had appeared on her forehead. I had seen enough TV crime shows to recognise the sniper's aiming marks. I didn't want her shot, as I hoped her story would work in her favour with a jury. Hoping I could prevent her death I jumped up and rushed to the window shouting, "Don't shoot!" and watched in horror as the glass shattered.

When the Police rushed into the room, they found me lying on the floor cradling her lifeless body.

David Swinton

To bake or not to bake... that is the question

I felt like some cake... not literally I don't mean. I may be soft and squidgy (possibly sometimes sweet, haha!) but that's not quite what I meant.

I fancied some cake... No, I hadn't seen a handsome hunk of cake walk past, nor a French fancy come to that.

It's just that I felt the need to eat some cake. Wrong on so many counts, I know, but sometimes a little of what you fancy does you good... And yes, we're still talking about cake here.

So, did I go out and buy some? Did I fiddle! Even though I've not made cake for years, unless you count banana bread (which everybody made in lockdown so it seems) or my healthy, not sweet, porridgey non-flapjacks... I intended to make a proper cake!

Easy peasy...bring it on...what can go wrong?!

I collected together (even weighed!) all the ingredients. How much sugar??!!! Well, I'm not putting all that in...half will do, and I'm using dark muscovado instead of soft light brown. I always think it gives a nicer flavour and doesn't seem as sweet. Feel free to disagree, you readers (is anybody really going to want to read this? I somehow doubt it...maybe if they like a bit of cake? Tim!)

Rightio. Here we go.

Bung... sorry, place... all the dry ingredients in a bowl.

In another bowl mix the oil and eggs [more washing up!]

Mix wet into dry... see, I could have used just one bowl, Delia, couldn't I?!

Anyway, chuck in... sorry, add... the carrots (grated into yet another bowl) and nuts and raisins (from a little dish)

All this blooming washing up!

Dollop... no, spoon... the mixture into a greased container (tin or wibbly wobbly silicon)

Put tin in preheated oven (or air fryer in my case) and BAKE!

20 minutes later, yummy smell wafting around, sweet and spicy, cakey, bakey smell.

Check it... Not quite done, sticky skewer, 5 more minutes.

Yay! It's done! Looks and smells 'grate' (grate! get it, carrot cake!)

First carrot cake for years.

Tip onto cooling rack.

Wiggle and tap container and out it flops.

Oh s**t! Bottom bit is left in tin... Oh well most of it is whole. Scrape the crumbs into a dish. Go to move the cake onto another surface...

Whoops! Catch the rack on edge of surface...cake breaks and half ends on the floor. Aieee!

Ah well, I shouldn't really be eating cake anyway, and the Monday group won't miss it as I haven't told them they were getting it.

It was a lovely carrot cake. I saved a couple of chunks to eat... it can't be sliced as it's in bits.

The birds have had a happy feast on the majority of it.

Who knew birds ate carrots!

Diane Gough

French Fried

"Waiter, I asked, indeed demanded, your finest table. You have stuck us in the darkest corner with only a view of the Opera House. As to the table itself, it's seventies kitsch. Stainless steel legs and an oak veneer top. Whatever next, table cloths? Anyway, I'm going to order for both of us. I'm sure Bethany here won't mind. After all, I am immeasurably rich both financially and in every other way. As you can no doubt tell I'm also incredibly suave and sophisticated, my accent alone could cut glass with a diamond or is it diamond with a glass? I can never remember which. So, from this shambles of a menu here, we'll have two Pate Maison followed by Lamb en Croute. As to vegetables I assume your French fries are edible, this being a French restaurant? Also bring aubergine and eggplant along with zucchini and courgette. Believe me, I'll know if you miss anything out. A bottle of your finest champagne oh, and some water for the table, the wood looks a little dry so we must pour some on poste haste. Now a word of warning, don't think chef can hide any snails or bits of frog under the jus, I'm on to you people. Off you go with all speed my good man, we haven't got all day. Right Belinda down to business, although why we're talking in a French restaurant I don't understand. After all the French have no word for Entrepreneur you know. However, I believe you want to borrow some money for a special project. Now ordinarily I don't do loans but, in your case, I might make an exception if you consent to be my fourth wife. I will of course square it with the other three first, they can get a little tetchy.

You know one of them even accused me of making up every word that comes out of my mouth, can you believe that Bridgette? Finally, here's the champagne. Well pour it quickly garcon, we're trying to close a deal. Bernadette, a toast to us. Ah, I imagine you pouring it over my head means you'll want some time to think about your answer. No, don't get up and storm out. Alright then if you insist, just give me a bell when you've mulled things over. Don't take too long though, time and tide...well you know the rest. Now, plate captain, hurry along with my food I'm even more ravenous than ever. Cancel the zucchini whilst you're about it, I'll just make do with courgette."

Timothy Webb

After Three ...

We're trying something new today, choir.
The basses go lower, the sopranos higher.
Altos, do your best.
Has everyone got a copy and a pen?
Erm, I don't want to have to ask again.
Altos, quiet. Please.
I'll pick out the tune with one finger.
Daisy, it's fine. You're a lovely singer.
Well, join the altos.
Where's Joe? He does steady the basses.
Oh, he's always away to exotic places.
Isn't Sandra an alto?
Can we step up practice to two a week. Please?
Yes, we want it ready for the pie and peas.
Altos, what's the matter?
Yes, it's a shock about Sandra and Joe.
We don't have all the facts, you know.
What do you mean, another alto?
Who? Elspeth? Yes, I suppose it's strange.
Joe must like them with their voice mid-range.
A united front. Altos.
Sopranos, lovely, if a little shrill.
But those high notes do give us a thrill.
Altos, forget about Sandra.
Tenors, your tone was nice and mellow.
You always thought Joe was a dodgy fellow?

Altos, you must stop assaulting the tenors.
Choir, you must have some decorum.
The practice is turning into a scrum.
Parts, please, altos, concentrate.
Ok, everyone. We have two choices.
Both these songs do suit our voices.
What's funny, altos?
Ok. "Love is all around me" is one.
What's that you're singing, Marion?
No, don't stop. Just carry on.
"Joe felt it with his fingers, and felt it with his toes"
Alright, altos. Keep it clean!
After three…

Loraine Rutherford

Armistice

Jeff handed Sal the mug decorated with the twelve days of Christmas. "Here's a cup of tea, love; might as well grab a few minutes before they arrive. The turkey is nearly done and Jimmy is riding his new bike with Kyle, who also got a bike for Christmas. Kyle's dad is watching them- avoiding the mother-in-law!"

Sal took another grateful sip of her tea." Don't mention mothers. Do you think that this year they will manage to get through the day without nearly starting WWIII between them?"

"If they do it will be a miracle. They have sniped at each other for the last 13 years," replied Jeff wearily.

Sal's mother had always thought that Jeff was not good enough for her daughter. She had dreamt of Sal marrying a doctor or solicitor, not a self-employed plumber. Jeff's mother regarded Carol, Sal's mother, as a snob. Her son was the apple of her eye and no-one was going to look down on him.

At 12 noon on the dot the doorbell rang. Sal heard Jeff welcome his parents while she finished changing into a long sleeved, fitted purple dress and some crystal drop earrings. Admittedly it was soon to be covered by a snowman apron but she liked to dress up at Christmas; she had not become a fan of the Christmas jumper. In addition, Jeff's parents would be formally dressed, as would her parents; although she suspected that there was an element of competition going on.

"Merry Christmas, Mavis, Frank," said Sal as she kissed them both.

"I see that your parents aren't here yet," noted Mavis. "Punctuality is so important."

Sal groaned inwardly. Her parents were always late and they played into Mavis' hands.

Fifteen minutes later the doorbell chime reverberated down the hall heralding the arrival of Sal's parents, Carol and Mike. Jeff ushered them into the living room.

"Happy Christmas," Carol and Mike uttered as they embraced their in-laws. Mavis scrutinized Carol from head to toe.

"My, that's a bright red dress. You wouldn't look out of place in the Market Square with all the other Christmas decorations."

Carol pursed her lips. "You look lovely in it," jumped in Jeff.

Frank caught Sal's eye and mouthed, "She's in a mood." Sal raised her eyes and sighed heavily. Fortunately, Carla entered the room and provided the necessary distraction. She was both sets of grandparents' only granddaughter and clearly a source of joy to them all.

Listening to Jimmy and Carla's stories about school, Christmas parties and presents ensured an enjoyable start to the meal. Calm waters remained during most of the main course with only a slight ripple over the turkey.

"This turkey is beautifully cooked, Sal," commented Carol.

"Thanks, but it is Jeff you have to thank for that."

"I thought as much. My Jeff always does everything right," declared Mavis.

"Sal is an excellent cook," retorted Carol.

"Not as...."

"Anyone for more wine?" interrupted Jeff.

By the time they got to puddings, a couple of bottles of wine had been consumed. Mavis had supplied the sherry trifle and Carol had made a Christmas pudding. It was customary for everyone to have a bit of everything. "Wow, Mum this sherry trifle packs a punch. Kids don't eat too much of it."

"I find that if you drench a trifle with too much sherry, it spoils it. You should be able to taste the other ingredients as well," commented Carol.

"I find," mimicked Mavis "that if you include too many raisins in a Christmas pudding it becomes gritty."

"Those raisins are Waitrose's best!"

"Both are lovely. Please just eat and enjoy," begged a flustered Sal.

Feeling stuffed to the gills, after a hefty meal, they all retired to the lounge. The low, weak sun was casting rays through the bay window and landing on Carol.

"That sun is bringing out your grey highlights perfectly," observed Mavis.

"I see that you haven't had your hair professionally coloured, yet. Still preferring the home pack? The trouble with those is that they tend to give an all-over flat colour, which isn't natural. The colours are also often darker than they say on the box; dark tones can be very ageing," fired back Carole.

Ceasefire ensued for a moment.

"Jimmy, Carla, come here I have a couple of presents for you," instructed Carol.

"Oh Mum, no! You have already spoilt them too much."

"If I can't spoil my grandchildren, who can I spoil?"

Carol handed Jimmy a large parcel. He ripped it open and shrieked when he saw a Liverpool United football strip with the top sporting the number of his favourite player. "Wow! That's great! THANKS". Carol then handed Carla her present. Carla's eyes lit up when she opened up the glossy, red vanity case to reveal a host of makeup.

"Mum. She is too young for makeup."

"Nonsense, Sal. It is all in neutral colours and is a good introduction."

"Thanks, Gran. It's fab."

Mavis had sat very quietly but she was not to be outdone. "Here, Jimmy and Carla, come and take these." Sal raised her eyes towards Jeff. All that could be heard was the tearing of paper until "Yippee, Wow, Great" burst forth from Jimmy. He held up a set of cricket whites including shin pads.

"I know that Jimmy doesn't play cricket yet but you were always really good at it, Jeff and he takes after you. Plus, they are starting up a junior team next Spring at the community centre. We think that he will really enjoy it."

Carla sat quietly staring at a voucher. "I thought that you could enjoy doing some shopping in the precinct." Carla could not take her eyes off the £50 on the receipt. She had never had so much money in one go. She leapt up and gave Mavis a huge hug and kiss. Mavis beamed.

With all the excitement over, Carla retreated to her bedroom to recommence texting friends and Jimmy somehow managed to persuade Sal and Jeff to let him ride his bike with Kyle. "It will be dark soon, Jimmy so no more than 20 minutes outside and keep in the cul-de-sac where we can see you. Understood?" When the children had left, there was a brooding silence in the room but not for long. Mavis threw a hand grenade at Carol who obliged by returning the same. Heavy, lengthy exchanges of gun fire increased in rapidity between them, with the odd bomb dropped for good measure. Sal had to take shelter in the kitchen. It was only when she was in there that she noticed how dark it had become and Jimmy had not yet appeared. She was about to put on her coat when there was frantic thumping on the front door. Kyle's father stood at the other side.

"Sal, come quickly. It's Jimmy. He is hurt. Pam is with him at the moment and we have rung for an ambulance." Before he had finished speaking, Sal was running down the road. She discovered that she could almost fly, as her feet seemed to glide inches above the pavement and covered the distance with astonishing ease. She saw a small bundle lying in the road.

"Sal, don't move him," yelled Jeff, as he followed behind.

She gazed at the pale, small face haloed by a crimson pool of blood. He was out cold. Sal stifled the urge to scream and was distracted by the piercing siren and cold shafts of blue light intruding the darkness. She watched them strap him on a stretcher; he looked even more vulnerable. "You go in the ambulance, Sal. I'll follow by car," instructed Jeff.

"Some teenagers on motorbikes had been terrorising Kyle and Jimmy. From what Kyle's dad could make out in between Kyle's sobs, Jimmy panicked and lost his balance. He and a motorbike collided." Sal just nodded as Jeff spoke but her eyes did not leave the bed where Jimmy lay still in a coma. He was so small, fragile and pale. His freckles stood out like stars on a dark, clear night. Her heart ached badly.

"If our son dies, those two will never darken our doors again," she uttered with furious resolve. "If we had not been caught up in their stupid arguing, we would have noticed that Jimmy had not come home and this could have been prevented!" Jeff merely put his head in his hands.

The night seemed endless as they slept fitfully in the large plastic armchairs. A nurse brought them some blankets and Jeff kept them supplied with dishwasher tasting coffee in plastic cups and tepid food from the canteen. Most were left hardly touched. Doctors and nurses kept checking on Jimmy throughout the night and the following morning but there was no change. By mid-afternoon, the nurse had suggested that they go home for some rest. Sal was resolute that she was not moving from Jimmy's side but exhaustion meant that she could not fight Jeff's insistence for long.

As they were leaving the hospital, they bumped into both sets of parents. Sal glared at Jeff. "You asked them?!"

"You need rest, Sal, even if it is just a few hours. Carla is at her friend's house and is having a sleep over," half whispered Carol.

When Jeff and Sal arrived home, they entered a spotless house and found two plates of meals in the fridge with instructions for heating them in the microwave. Jeff persuaded Sal to try and sleep and as soon as her head hit the pillow, she descended into oblivion for four hours. Sal woke suddenly and for the thirty seconds she was at peace but then the realisation of what had happened bulldozed itself into her consciousness. She leapt out of bed, soaked herself in the falling, hot water of the shower and scrubbed as if to remove the contamination of the accident. Once dressed in more comfortable clothes for the hospital, she went down stairs to find Jeff at the breakfast bar with two hot plates of food waiting for them. Despite the constant nausea that she felt, Sal was surprised how much she was enjoying the meal until Jimmy came to mind and the trap door in her stomach instantly shut.

Sal took the stairs up to the ward two at a time. She no longer could repeat her flying sensation, in fact she felt that she was dragging two large boulders with her, but determination drove her on. On the way to Jimmy's room, she glanced into the visitors' waiting room to see which set of parents was in there. Sal was surprised to see Frank and Mike. "Where are Mum and Mavis?"

"In with Jimmy, love."

"What? You have left them together with my ill child? He needs peace." At that Sal sprinted to his room. She glanced in through the viewing window and was stunned to see her mother and Mavis hugging each other. Jeff joined her just as she was about to open the door.

"Don't. Give them another ten minutes."

When they returned to Jimmy's room, Carol and Mavis were at either side of his bed holding his hands. Both looked as if they had been crying.

"Has anything happened?" asked Sal.

"No, love. Jimmy is just the same but I am sure that he will be OK. He is a little fighter."

Carol and Mavis never told anyone what happened between them when they were alone with Jimmy. They had sat in silence holding his hands but the silence was productive. Eventually, Mavis said "Sal, is a good wife and mother."

"Yes," replied Carol," and Jeff is a good husband and father. He does you proud." Silence descended again until Carol heard a noise coming from Mavis. She looked up and Mavis was sobbing with her head in her hands. Carol walked to the other side of the bed and threw her arms around her.

"We are stupid, old women," cried Mavis. "How could we have behaved the way we have all these years? If anything happens to that boy, I will never forgive myself and neither will Sal. I saw the way she looked at us earlier today."

Carol sighed, "Yes. And she is my daughter. I don't want to lose her." She paused. "Why is it that we only seek peace when the suffering becomes too great? Why can't we see what others see before it gets to that point? We have to stop."

Jeff and Sal took over the night duty and followed their routine from the previous evening. Despite the discomfort of trying to sleep in the chair, Sal succumbed to sleep and dreamt that Jimmy was calling her. The call became so persistent that she woke with a start. It was only then, that she saw her son with his eyes open, hoarsely calling "Mum, Mum." Jeff would tell people later that Sal's shriek woke every patient in the hospital and that she nearly smothered Jimmy to death. From that moment on, the room was abuzz with doctors and nurses. Over the next few days, Jimmy underwent numerous tests and to everyone's relief, there was no lasting damage.

It was Christmas Day and Jeff rang the doorbell at his parents' house. The door opened to the sound of soothing music and female laughter coming from the kitchen. Mike and Frank were seated in the living room with a beer each and Carol and Mavis were creating a joint Christmas meal. Jimmy was wearing his Liverpool top and cricket bottoms and Carla looked pretty with her expertly applied subtle toned makeup. Mavis came in to the living room with a tray of drinks. "A toast," she said.

"Merry Christmas."

"Cheers."

"A lasting armistice!"

Christine McCluskey

Christmas

My neighbour hurt himself today
Pulling Christmas crackers
He pulled too hard, his hand slipped off
And hit him in his,,, mouth

The presents all are purchased
No one has been excluded
All I can do is hope that none come
Batteries excluded

The presents are all bought and wrapped
I hope there's nothing wrong
I should be ok after all
It's all rubbish from Hong Kong

My present for my mother-in-law
Could not possibly be finer
Beautiful piece of Christmas tat
Manufactured in China

Christmas comes but once a year
For that let's all raise a cheer
It used to last two days at most
These days, two months, I fear

In days of yore
The Christmas joy

Was seen in children's eyes
Pity then the whole damned thing
Is now commercialised

The turkey and the trimmings
Are eaten up with glee
But surely no one likes the sprouts
It can 't be only me

Turkey with the trimmings
A meal bound to impress
Pity nearly all the guests
Have been drinking to excess

David Swinton

Friendship

Thanks for the good times
And showing me, what life really means,
Without you I would have slipped into a shell
Like the hermit crab.
He needs no one, only his own company
Unlike us, who need friends.

On our first meeting, I was shy
Then as our friendship grew, so
I grew out of that solitary shell
Which held me for so long.
I hope we'll never have to say goodbye
Last farewells are hard.

Our parting now is only temporary.
Even if we never meet again, we'll
Still remain in each other's minds.
Put pen to paper and keep in touch.

Kathleen Little

Acknowledgements

Our sincere thanks go, once again, to **David Wise**, the Librarian at Lynemouth, who continues to patiently facilitate our sessions, provide us with tea and lots of encouragement.

Authors' Biographies

Emma Eyers

Emma only joined the group this year, but has been writing for fun since she was a teenager. She takes her inspiration from animals, the countryside around her, historic events and the challenges set by the group.

Diane Gough

Diane...who only came to make up the numbers...still enjoying trying to write...with the help of Sophie 🐩 ...and of course, her infamous (or naughty!) dots... 😏 ...

Christine McCluskey

Christine McCluskey started writing, something she had wanted to do for years, when retirement and lockdown coincided. However, it was not until she joined Lynemouth Library Writing Group that she found encouragement and challenge to write regularly. Christine loves playing with words and ideas.

Betty Mitcheson

Betty, having done very little writing since school days and thinking her work wouldn't be good enough, rather reluctantly joined this writing group at the ripe old age of 78! However, they have given her the inspiration and encouragement to write her stories, mostly from life, and even poems.

Kathleen Little

Kath has been writing since she was a teenager and takes inspiration from events, memories and her childhood in Gloucestershire. After attending a presentation by the writing group in Ellington, she was invited by Loraine to join.

Loraine Rutherford

Loraine continues to enjoy her writing, especially poetry. She has been involved in an Open Mic event and reading some of her work to community groups, to which she feels her style of writing lends itself.

David Swinton

Once retirement took hold, David felt the need to continue expressing himself, so embraced writing and joined the writer's group. He now spends - possibly too many - hours assaulting his keyboard. When asked what is his style, he is happy to leave the decision on that up to the reader!

Chris Waterson

Chris has written everything from poetry to pantomime and self-published two anthologies and a short novel, but derives the greatest pleasure from sharing efforts and drawing inspiration from the authors of this book.

Timothy Webb

Having arrived in Lynemouth four years ago Timothy (Tim) revels in the beauty of Northumberland's coast and countryside. Writing now mostly for cathartic purposes, he is always pleased and amazed when others find it tolerable. His writing style has been described as eclectic. He is still to discover what this means.

Elaine B Wilson

Elaine draws inspiration for her fast fiction from everyday life. She explores themes of love, loss, hope and transformation which hopefully leaves readers with a sense of connection to the characters and their journeys.

Printed in Dunstable, United Kingdom